LANDGRABBERS

LANDGRABBERS

DAN J. STEVENS

CENTER POINT LARGE PRINT
THORNDIKE, MAINE

This Center Point Large Print edition
is published in the year 2024 by arrangement with
Golden West Inc.

Originally published in the US by Belmont Books.

The text of this Large Print edition is unabridged.
In other aspects, this book may vary
from the original edition.
Printed in the United States of America
on permanent paper sourced using
environmentally responsible foresting methods.
Set in 16-point Times New Roman type.

ISBN: 979-8-89164-277-5

The Library of Congress has cataloged this record
under Library of Congress Control Number: 2024938122

LANDGRABBERS

CHAPTER I

Deputy John Lund stood on a small rise of ground twenty feet from the edge of the crowd, his gaze on Chauncey Ryan, who was at one end of the so-called wheel of fortune, and his daughter Babs, on the other.

High-flaming torches at the corners of the platform gave it a weird appearance of light and shadow and drifting smoke. All it would take to complete Johnny's mental picture of hell would be a few devils with pitchforks in their hands standing behind Ryan and the girl.

Johnny was scared. He couldn't put his finger on what scared him. It wasn't the giant land lottery that was being held here on the south shore of Mallard Lake, or Chauncey Ryan, though the man was formidable enough, and it certainly was not the girl Babs.

Johnny didn't know any of the people in the crowd well enough to be scared of them, not even the half-dozen gunmen who stood next to the platform. They looked tough, but he knew he could handle them if it came to that. Gunmen were as human as anyone. It was the unknown that he couldn't handle, the unpredictable, and right now he couldn't even guess what was going to happen.

He watched Ryan give the wheel of fortune a whirl. It wasn't really a wheel at all, but a metal drum that reminded him of a barrel drum. Inside were thousands of tiny pieces of paper, each with a number on it. Behind Babs on a small stand was a giant fish bowl containing more pieces of paper with the names of people who had bought tickets which guaranteed a piece of land for each ticket.

A huge map of the Cascade and Snake River Wagon Road Grant stood upright on the rear of the platform. Lines marked off plots of land which varied in size from ten acres to the sprawling Cross Heart twenty miles to the north. Each piece of land was numbered.

The procedure was for Babs to draw a name from the fish bowl, then take a number from the wheel of fortune. Ryan would match the number with the plot of land on the map having the same number. The person whose name Babs had drawn received the land that was matched in this manner.

"Ladies and gentlemen," Ryan was saying in his booming voice as he gave the wheel of fortune another whirl, "I welcome you to the second night of the drawing for land and fortune here on the shores of beautiful Lake Mallard. Today we sold more than two hundred tickets. As you know, every one of them guarantees you a piece of land somewhere in the Cascade and Snake River Wagon Road Grant.

"The company does not guarantee you a ranch or a townsite or a stream of flowing water. Whether you win such a valuable prize is the chance you take. Most of you know this, but for those of you who arrived today in our fair city, and believe me, Mallard City will be a fair city of stone and lumber within a matter of months and not one of tents as it is tonight, I want to tell you that in this grant there is one huge cattle ranch known as the Cross Heart. Some lucky person will own that ranch by next Sunday night. This ranch will not be cut up and sold in small parcels of land, but will be handed over intact to the man or woman, the boy or girl, who draws the lucky number."

Ryan motioned toward the map. "The number is 49. Keep it in mind, ladies and gentlemen. One of you will draw that number. In one brief instant that person will be wealthy. I hesitate to tell you how wealthy because you would not believe it. All I can say is that the stock and machinery and buildings will be turned over to the new owner exactly as they are today, lock, stock and barrel.

"If you haven't seen the Cross Heart, get on your horse and ride up there tomorrow and look at it, then come back and purchase another ticket or ten more tickets or one hundred. Buy as many as you can afford. We have less than ninety left unsold. The price is $100 a ticket. I need not point out to you that the more tickets you own, the better chance you have of drawing the Cross Heart."

Ryan reached out and whirled the wheel of fortune again. "Now, besides the Cross Heart, there are any number of sizable parcels that are large enough to support a man and family. Ten acres. One hundred acres. Five hundred acres. Some of these pieces of land have fine timber on them that is worth a fortune. I assure you that within six months . . . a year . . ." He spread his hands. "Who knows when, but soon a railroad will be extended north across the California-Oregon line to tap this great resource. For those of you who own timber, it will be exactly the same as taking a check to the bank to be cashed."

Ryan stepped forward to the edge of the platform and, removing his hat, wiped his forehead with a red bandanna. He was a showman, Johnny told himself resentfully, a showman who twisted the truth but not enough to be called a downright liar.

Johnny had lived in this country all of his life. He was twenty-one years old, and railroad talk had been in the air every one of those years. Still, the rails had not crossed the state line. More than that, Johnny doubted that ten pieces of land in the entire wagon road grant had enough timber to make anyone a fortune.

"Now then, ladies and gentlemen," Ryan continued, "Let me give you one more item of information. In addition to the Cross Heart and the timber land, there are a number of fresh water streams crossing the grant, many of them large enough to furnish water for irrigation. Some of the other pieces of land lie over underground lakes, so it is only a matter of digging a well to get the water you need. Also, with every tenth number that is drawn, a lot here in Mallard City will be given as a bonus to that lucky person.

"I know some of you have come many miles and have been disappointed in what you see here. I ask you to have patience. The day of fulfillment is at hand. This country which you see as a sagebrush desert today will blossom like a rose tomorrow. I suggest that the Garden of Eden may have looked like this before Adam put his hand to the plow, before he cut his timber, before the railroad came, and before he dug his irrigation ditches. All it takes is time and work, and I know enough of you men personally to be convinced that you will work."

A showman and a salesman, Johnny told himself. Chauncey Ryan could take a broken-down, twenty-year-old nag and sell him as a frisky three-year-old. Johnny hated to admit it, but the man did have an appeal.

Chauncey Ryan was handsome and bronze-skinned, probably in his mid-thirties, a good six feet tall and broad of shoulder. He wore a calfskin vest over a bright blue silk shirt, buckskin pants encased in expensive black boots, a broad-brimmed white hat, and a pearl-handled .45 in a black holster.

His daughter Babs was a vital part of the team. She was sixteen or seventeen, Johnny guessed, blond and blue-eyed, and not over five feet tall. Her features were good, her smile quick and natural. There was something else about her that had made Johnny like her the first time he'd seen her, a quality he couldn't quite name, but he guessed it was the love of life as much as anything. He had a notion she felt she might not be around very long and she intended to make the most of every hour she had on this good earth.

Ryan continued to extoll the virtues and the possibilities of the land the ticket-holders would receive. He was, of course, hoping to sell the rest of the tickets, but now that the suckers—and that was exactly what they were in Johnny's opinion—were here and could look at the land they were buying, selling more tickets to them was a difficult if not an impossible task.

Johnny's gaze swept the crowd, the scared feeling in him growing until it squeezed his belly and worked up into his chest so that he found it hard to breathe. Suddenly he knew. The crowd wasn't just a group of over five hundred men and women. It was a monster—a great, sullen beast made up of people who had come in wagons and stagecoaches and on horses hundreds and even thousands of miles, people who had used most of their savings to buy tickets, expecting to draw good land they could farm. Many of them were broke, some even hungry, and all were disillusioned, angry people who had expected something for nothing and now knew that only a few would receive anything worthwhile.

"We come to the time, ladies and gentlemen," Ryan was saying, "when we start the drawing of the evening. We will pick ten names tonight just as we did last night, and we will do the same every night throughout the week. On Saturday and Sunday we will start the drawing in the mornings and continue all day. We expect to be finished by sundown Sunday. Sometime before that we will know the names of new owners of the Cross Heart and the other choice parcels of land."

Chauncey Ryan wasn't very smart, Johnny thought, or he wouldn't try to keep selling tickets to these people. Most of them didn't have any money, and all of them were sour-tempered because the salesmen who had fanned out over the United States to sell the tickets had misrepresented the country and the average size of the plots of land.

Ryan gave the wheel of fortune another whirl as he shouted, "All right, let's find out whose name comes up first. No one knows where the wheel of fortune will stop. No one knows whose name will be plucked from all these thousands of names by the nimble fingers of Babs Ryan."

Johnny took a deep breath, forcing his taut muscles to suck air into his lungs. He looked at the crowd in front of the platform, at the dark, unshaven faces of men who had held high hopes before they came, and the women with sun bonnets tied around their hair, their faces showing weariness from the long journey that had brought them here.

Johnny saw resentment on their faces, a smoldering anger, a sullen hatred for this smooth-tongued man with the wide-brimmed, white hat. Still, it wasn't so much what Johnny saw as what he felt, a queer, abnormal tension that had welded these people into the monster that the crowd had become.

Babs dipped her hand into the fish bowl and drew out a slip of paper. Ryan took it, glanced at it, and read, "Al Dillon." He nodded at the girl. "Now let's see if Mr. Dillon is the lucky one. Draw his number, Babs."

Johnny knew Al Dillon. He had been one of the first to arrive in a covered wagon from the Rogue River valley on the other side of the Cascade mountains. His daughter Ann had come with him, a tall, graceful girl who had somehow retained her faith in the future, although it was plain enough to Johnny that her father was another dreamer, a drifter, a man who had chased rainbows all of his life.

Dillon was standing at the edge of the crowd. Ann was not with him. She was probably back at the camp, Johnny thought, sewing patches on patches so her father would have another pair of pants he could wear. Dillon was a gaunt, hungry-looking man with a down-turned mustache and slumped shoulders and the manner of one who has been beaten into subjection by the adversities of life.

Now he straightened and moved a couple of steps toward Johnny so that he stood alone. For this one, short moment he was bright with hope as Babs handed her father a piece of paper from the wheel of fortune.

Hope for Al Dillon lasted not more than the few seconds it took Ryan to look at the number and glance at the map behind him. He shook his head and shouted, "103. I'm sorry, Mr. Dillon. You drew ten acres of land north of here, one mile from the lake. I guess this isn't your lucky night." Ryan gave the metal drum another whirl. "We'll try again. No one knows where the wheel of fortune will stop. No one knows . . ."

Johnny had been watching Dillon. He saw the despair that engulfed the man and took the starch out of his shoulders. Johnny knew exactly how he felt, the dream that had given him hope for so long burned into nothingness in those few seconds.

Now Dillon cried out, an involuntary sound that was wordless. He yanked a revolver from his waistband and leveled it at Ryan as he yelled, "You damned thief. I'm going to kill you."

Johnny leaped at the man, all the time knowing he was a second too late.

CHAPTER II

Johnny heard the roar of the gun, he had the impression that Chauncey Ryan had fallen to the floor of the platform, then he had Al Dillon by the waist and had pulled him to the ground. They rolled over once, Johnny keeping a tight grip on the man. Dillon tried to fight; he kicked and struck Johnny with his fists, yelling that he had to kill the son of a bitch.

They rolled over once more, and this time when Johnny came on top, he loosened his grip and slugged Dillon on the jaw. The man went limp. For a moment Johnny wasn't sure whether he was knocked cold or had simply given up. He picked up the revolver Dillon had dropped and was on his hands and knees when he realized that the six gunmen who had been lined along the edge of the platform were coming toward him, the one named Plug Tully in the lead.

Johnny rose to his feet, the gun still in his hand. He would not have been surprised if the crowd had rolled over him like a tidal wave and had taken Dillon away from him; he was surprised that the gunmen were buying into this.

"Thanks for keeping him from killing Ryan," Tully said. "We'll take him now."

Johnny was surprised and shocked. He asked, "You'll take him where?"

"To the nearest pine tree that has a strong enough limb to hold him," Tully said. "Step away."

Plug Tully had stopped ten feet from Johnny; the other five were divided, three on one side of Tully and two on the other. Johnny said, "No, I'm not stepping away. He's my prisoner. If you did hang him, I'd arrest the bunch of you for murder."

Tully laughed without humor. "Would you now, sonny? Don't bet too much on that. Just because you've got your star all polished up bright and shiny don't mean you can handle the likes of us."

"I can handle you, all right," Johnny said. "If any of you try to draw or rush me, I'll put a window in your skull right between your eyes, Tully. Now get to hell out of here so I can take my prisoner to jail."

Plug Tully was the youngest of the lot, Johnny guessed, and he also guessed that the man was toughest and meanest. The six were a good deal alike. The difference was simply that Tully was more so, more humorless, more barren-faced, colder and more calloused than the others.

For a time none of the six moved or spoke. They stared at Johnny and he stared at Plug Tully, the gun in his hand lined on Tully's forehead. Johnny had heard once that there were men who loved death, who are like dogs that roll in the decayed and stinking flesh of dead animals. These men were like that. They had been hired to kill, and now it seemed to Johnny that the smell of death hung over them.

But Plug Tully did not favor death for himself. He said finally, "All right, Lund. There'll be another time. Right now you'd better keep one idea in your head. We've been hired by the company to protect company men. If you don't let us do it, you'll pay for every company man this bunch of punkin rollers murder."

They wheeled and strode back toward the platform. Chauncey Ryan had gotten to his feet holding one hand in the air. "Ladies and gentlemen, that puts an end to the drawing for tonight. I will not stand up here before you and be a clay pigeon. If I am shot at again, I will pack up and leave. You'll be camped here for a month before the wagon road grant company sends another man to continue the drawing, if it sends anybody at all. Now go on back to your camps."

The crowd made a strange sound, a sort of rumbling roar that reminded Johnny again of a great beast. The men and women who made up the crowd were humans; the crowd was not. Johnny hauled Dillon to his feet and prodded him in the back with the muzzle of his own gun.

"Git," Johnny said softly. "Down the road to the jail. You make a wrong move and I'll blow your backbone apart."

Johnny would not have been surprised by anything that happened now. The six gunmen were lined up again along the front of the platform, their cold eyes on the crowd, their hands on the butts of their guns.

If the gunmen had not taken the position they had, the crowd might have become a mob and rolled forward, destroying everything in front of it, killing Ryan and the girl, too. But no one took the lead, no one had the courage to buck the gunmen, so nothing happened.

When they were fifty yards down the road, Dillon muttered, “I did the wrong thing, didn’t I?”

“You sure did,” Johnny said. “If you’d killed Ryan, you’d have swung for murder. As it is, you’ll go to the pen for attempted murder.”

Dillon groaned. “What will happen to Ann?”

“She might be better off without you,” Johnny said. “Ever think of that?”

“Yes, I’ve thought of it,” Dillon said, and began to cry.

Johnny was filled with revulsion. It wasn’t just that Al Dillon was weak. He wallowed in it. How he’d ever had enough nerve to pull his gun and take a shot at Ryan was more than Johnny could understand, but he had heard the sheriff, Ed Neal, say more than once that weak and cowardly men are often more dangerous than stronger, braver ones.

The main street of the tent city lay ahead of them. Here was a store, a post office, a telegraph office, two big tents with cots that were hotels for men, two restaurants, four saloons and gambling places, three tent livery stables, and two brothels at the far end of the street.

There were no accommodations for women. Now, with her father in jail, Ann would have to do for herself. She had the team and wagon and whatever supplies there were in the wagon, and probably not one cent of money.

Mallard City had sprung up within the last week as the ticket owners had arrived. It was strung out along the wagon road that led north, the road following the east side of Mallard Lake for ten miles and running on to Piute, the county seat, which was eighty miles beyond the northern tip of the lake.

A ranch had had its headquarters here in the early days when the cattle business had been better. The house still stood, a weather-beaten, two-story structure that had never seen a drop of paint. The windows had been broken, the doors removed by settlers, and a lean-to room on the back had been completely torn down and the lumber stolen. The company had repaired the house and it was being used by Chauncey Ryan and George Mandell, one of the owners of the company, as their office. Two of the three upstairs rooms were their bedrooms. The other belonged to Babs.

Besides the main house, one small stone structure survived. Johnny guessed it had been an office. It was strong and well built, the roof intact, with tiny windows higher than a man's head on two sides. The door was thick and solid, the hinges in good shape, so Johnny bought a padlock and put up a sign JAIL. He slept in a tent a few feet behind the building.

Johnny had not liked his assignment when the sheriff had given it to him, but he'd accepted it because he had no choice. Obviously some lawman had to be here during the drawing and the sheriff said he couldn't stay away from Piute that long.

Now, as he propelled Dillon toward the jail, he wondered if he should send for the sheriff. There would be hell to pay before long, and he didn't think any one man, no matter how good a man he was, could handle it.

Still, he hesitated. Ed Neal had made it plain he wouldn't be gone from Piute more than two or three days at a time, so it was up to Johnny to handle the situation if he wanted to keep his job. As he pushed Dillon through the door, the thought occurred to him that maybe he didn't want to keep this job.

No matter what happened, the law would be blamed for anything that went wrong, and he was the law. Chauncey Ryan had asked him that afternoon to send for the sheriff and he'd refused. Well, he'd refuse again, he thought, if Ryan pressed his demand.

"Go get Ann, will you?" Dillon asked. "I've got to see her."

"Sorry, but I can't leave here. Maybe she'll come when she hears what happened."

Johnny pulled the door shut and snapped the padlock, then stood listening as the crowd broke up. The couples returned to their camps, but most of the single men drifted along Main Street to the saloons. These men might be nearly broke, Johnny thought angrily, but the saloons and brothels would end up with the money they did have, and the rotgut whisky they bought would make his job tougher.

He stood there, listening to the rumble of talk as the men moved along the street. They were still angry and resentful, judging from the scraps of conversation that came to him. He wasn't sure that anyone could talk sense into them.

Someone else might try to do what Dillon had failed to do, although killing Chauncey Ryan was completely stupid. Killing the man would slow up the drawing just as he had said and accomplish nothing. Few of them had enough money or supplies to sit here and twiddle their thumbs while they waited for a new man to arrive.

A woman appeared out of the darkness, calling, "Mr. Lund!"

"Here," he said, walking to her but not recognizing her in the starlight until he was within a few feet of her. Then he saw that it was Ann

Dillon. "I'm glad you came. Your pa asked for you while ago, but I didn't want to leave."

"I'm glad you didn't leave," she said. "I'd like to talk to him."

"Use one of the windows," he said. "There's no glass in them. I won't search you. I don't think you'll try to pass a gun to him."

"Of course not," she said. "He's safer inside than out."

She moved around the corner to one of the windows. Johnny remained where he was, far enough away so he couldn't follow their talk. Then it stopped and a moment later she appeared around the corner of the building.

"I have something to tell you, Mr. Lund," the girl said. "I asked Pa to tell you, but he won't do it. He's mad because I'm going to tell, but you've got to know."

She hesitated, as if uncertain of her wisdom in telling what she had in mind. He said, "Go ahead. There may be more to this than I know about. It struck me as queer that your pa would try to shoot Ryan."

"It is," she said. "He doesn't even own a gun. I don't know who gave him the one he used. But that's part of what I want to tell you. Most of the ticket-holders are convinced they have no chance for the Cross Heart or even the timber land. I don't know how the rumor started, but they believe Ryan is rigging the drawing so he or someone he favors will get the good property. Men like my father and most of the others will end up with ten acres of worthless sagebrush-covered land."

"I can't do much about what they think," Johnny said. "Even if it was true, which I doubt, I couldn't do anything about it."

"Wait," she said. "Maybe you can do something about this. A few of the men want Ryan murdered. Mandell, too, I guess. They think new men will give them an honest draw. Pa failed, but one of the others will try. What worries me is that they may be so afraid he'll tell who they are that they'll kill him."

"Maybe you'd better tell me who they are," Johnny said. "I'll arrest them for conspiracy to murder or something like that."

"I can't tell you, Mr. Lund," she whispered. "I don't know. All I know is that there is such a plot. Will you protect him?"

"I'll do the best I can," Johnny said, "but I can't be here watching him all the time."

Without another word she whirled and ran. She was crying, he thought, and mentally cursed Al Dillon and the rest of them who had thought up this murderous scheme. There probably wasn't a bit of truth to the rumor about Ryan rigging the draw. But when he thought about it, he wasn't sure.

CHAPTER III

Chauncey Ryan was a badly frightened man. He sat at his desk in his office in the old ranch house, sweat pouring down his face, his stomach feeling as if it were glued to his backbone. He had been shot at before, but it had never made him feel like this.

He looked at Babs who sat in a rocking chair on the other side of the room. "The company hires six gunslicks to protect us," he said, "and the county's got a deputy around here somewhere, but still I get shot at."

Babs smiled as she rocked, the chair squeaking under her. "If the deputy hadn't been as quick as he was, you'd be dead right now," she said. "Just thank your lucky stars you're still alive, lover."

"Don't call me that down here where somebody can walk in and hear you," he said irritably.

"Well, I'll tell you one thing," she said. "I'm getting damned tired of this daughter role I'm playing. I'm used to taking a more interesting part."

"Same here," he grumbled, "but this will only go on until the end of the week. If everything works out, we'll ride out of here with a small fortune in the sock."

Babs looked down at her long, slender fingers,

skilled fingers that were adept at many things, from picking pockets to dealing cards from the bottom of a deck. She was here in Mallard City because of those fingers.

She was twenty-one, not sixteen as she wanted everyone to think. She was not the sweet, naive child she hoped people would take her for, either. Three years ago she had teamed up with Chauncey Ryan. They had made some money in those years, but nothing big. Now, as Chauncey said, they'd have the jackpot they wanted by the end of the week, if everything worked out. There always seemed to be an if.

She leaned forward and said in a low tone, "I've waited for that same small fortune ever since I heard your first rosy promise three years ago. Now it looks as if we might really get our hands on it. If you go yellow and walk out on the deal, I'll kill you. I'm not waiting for more promises."

He wiped his face with his bandanna. If a man had ever stepped right into a bear trap with his eyes wide open and got caught, he was the man.

"I'm not walking out on the deal," he said, "but I was the one who got shot at, not you, and I'm the one they'll shoot at again. If I'd known how crooked the company was in selling the tickets, I never would have taken this job in the first place."

She smiled again. "The company crooked? Well, look who's calling the kettle black."

"You run enough risks being crooked yourself," he said, "but when you come along behind a company and pick up the results of their crookedness, you're twice as bad off."

She shrugged. "We didn't look for a bed of roses when we took this job. Don't forget I'm on the same platform you are."

"But I'm the one they'll shoot at," he said.

"Maybe you're the one they'll shoot at," she said, "but if someone shows up out here who recognizes you or me, they'll lynch both of us."

He dismissed the possibility with a wave of his hand. "We always worked the Mississippi, and we've never been closer to Oregon than Missouri or Arkansas. That's a long ways from here."

"There's maybe five hundred men camped along this lake," she said, "and they've come from all over the United States. The odds are good that at least one of them has run into us somewhere."

"If he did, he might recognize me, but he wouldn't know you," Ryan said. "You've changed your hair and you're wearing different clothes and you've washed your face. Taking off that stuff you used to wear has made a hell of a good-looking woman out of you. Besides, any time you play for big stakes, you're going to run a risk."

"That's what I wanted to hear you say," she

said. “I’ve stuck with you for three years waiting for the big hand to be dealt us. Now that we’re holding it, I’m not going to let you throw it in.”

Chauncey Ryan took a cigar from his coat pocket, bit off the end, and studied the woman as he rolled it between his fingers. He had been on his own since he was thirteen years old; he had occasionally done some honest work during the twenty-two years since then, but most of the time he had lived off other people in one way or another. When he thought of some of his narrow escapes, he got the same queasy feeling in the pit of his stomach that he had now.

“Babs, this is our last caper,” he said. “Maybe having a legitimate business will be a dull way to live, but it’s a hell of a lot safer than the way we’ve been living. I’m willing to settle for a little dullness.”

“So am I,” Babs said.

“All right then,” Ryan said. “I’m scared, but I’m not going to throw this hand in. We’ll play it out.”

“Good,” she said. “It’s just that it seemed to me your backbone needed a little stiffening.”

He struck a match and held it to the tip of his cigar and pulled on it. When he had it going, he blew the match out and laid it in the ashtray on his desk. He was thinking about a little town that he and Babs had gone through on their way out here.

It was snuggled in a high, green valley in the Colorado Rockies, out of the way where no one would be likely to know them, good hunting and fishing, and it had a store that could be bought for $5,000. After they left here, they'd have enough money to buy the store and a house and furnish it, and maybe have some left over.

He blew out a long plume of smoke, smiling a little as he thought about it. He said, "You're right. All I've got to do is stay alive until we've pulled this job off Sunday night and collect from Tebo Rand."

She rose. "I'm going to bed. You coming in tonight?"

"I'd better not," he said. "Mandell's still out. We can't afford to do anything to start him guessing about us."

"I suppose not," she said, disappointed. "But it's like I said. I don't care much for the daughter role."

She turned toward the stairs, then stopped. Someone was coming in from the street. Chauncey heard it, too, and scooted back from his desk, his right hand gripping the butt of his gun. He kept his eyes on the door until George Mandell appeared out of the darkness, then he relaxed.

Mandell was a tall, very thin man, about sixty, with white hair, a white mustache, and a white goatee. He was one of the owners of the wagon road company, sent here by the other owners to see that the drawing was run properly. Ryan didn't like him, but he had to get along with him and so far he had. Now, looking at the man, he wasn't sure he was going to get along with him much longer. The man was furious.

"I just heard that you called off the drawing after you pulled one name," Mandell said. "For your information, you were hired to pull ten names every night until Saturday and Sunday."

Ryan took the cigar out of his mouth. This was typical of men who had money and hired other men to do their work. He said, "According to my information, you were sent here by the other owners of the company to be on hand when the drawings were made. Well, Mr. Mandell, where were you when that one name was pulled?"

The man's face turned red. He said, "It's none of your God-damned business where I was. You're here to take my orders, not to ask me questions."

"You'll have to answer some questions if I wire the other owners of the company about where you spend your time," Ryan said. "Maybe you didn't hear the rest of the story. One of the suckers, Al Dillon, shot at me tonight. I'd probably have been killed if that kid deputy Lund hadn't been on the job."

"You weren't hit," Mandell snapped. "Why didn't you go on with the drawing?"

"Because I don't propose to be a clay pigeon

for you or anybody else," Ryan said. "The company hired Plug Tully and his gunhands, but they didn't keep Dillon from taking a shot at me. Tomorrow night you're going to be on that platform with me, and then they'll have two clay pigeons if we've got some more killers in the crowd, and I'm guessing we have."

"Not me," Mandell said. "No reason for me to be on that platform."

"There's all the reason in the world," Ryan said. "Your crooked company misrepresented just about everything to the suckers when they sold the tickets. That's why they're sore. They're going to keep on being sore because they've been lied to and I guess you can't blame 'em much, but that's not the point. The point is you and me and maybe Babs are being blamed for the lies your salesmen told. We'll do well to get this job done and stay alive."

Some of the fury went out of Mandell. He stared at Ryan for a moment, then said, "With this kind of a crowd, we need the sheriff, not a deputy who's still wet behind the ears."

"The sheriff might help some things," Ryan conceded, "but what I'm telling you is that you're going to be on that platform with me from now on or there won't be any more drawing. It will be up to you whether we stop the drawing if one of us or Babs gets shot at."

Mandell took a long breath. He said, "All right,

but I'm going to wire the sheriff. He's got to be here tomorrow. This is an explosive situation, and it takes a cool head to keep that crowd from becoming a mob."

He turned and walked out of the house. Ryan chewed on his cigar and winked at Babs. "There you are, one of the country's great capitalists. He bought the wagon road grant for a song during the panic, and with a few other dollar grabbers, cooked up this scheme to get rid of it at a profit. Now that his lies are catching up with him, he wants the law to look out for him."

Babs walked to the desk. "Do you think the sheriff will come?"

"I don't know," Ryan answered. "I've never met the man." He tongued the cigar to the other side of his mouth. "Tebo Rand is the same breed of cat. He's so crooked he could lie in the shadow of a corkscrew, but once he gets the Cross Heart, he'll want the law to look out for his interest."

"I'm not going to worry about Tebo Rand's morals," Babs said. "He's paying us to rig the drawing for his benefit and that's good enough for me if he pays us off." She paused, frowning. "Chauncey, do you suppose Johnny Lund knows anything about the shooting?"

"Why should he?" Ryan asked. "I mean, a wild man loses his temper because he didn't hit the jackpot and tries to kill me. What's there for the deputy to know?"

“I’m not sure,” she said. “I guess I was asking if that’s all it was, just a wild man losing his temper. Or is there more to it?”

Ryan pulled on his cigar, the butterflies flapping in his stomach again. He knew what she meant. There might be a conspiracy. If so, someone else would try, now that Dillon had failed.

“He might,” Ryan said. “Go find out.”

“Now?” Babs asked. “Are you crazy? He’s asleep.”

“Wake him,” Ryan said. “Crawl into bed with him.”

“All right,” she said. “It sounds like an exciting idea. I’ll do it.”

CHAPTER IV

Tebo Rand was a schemer. He prided himself on the fact that he was not a two-bit tinhorn like Chauncey Ryan and the woman who called herself Babs. He was a solid citizen who made his money buying and selling anything from land and cattle and horses to a wagonload of cats that he hauled into the Colorado mining country and sold at a profit to the miners who were being overrun with rats.

No, Tebo Rand was not a tinhorn. He was a man who kept his eyes and ears open and, seeing an opportunity to make money, pursued that opportunity with every faculty he had. Sometimes he lost, but usually he won.

Win or lose, there was always the thrill of uncertainty, the thrill of pulling the necessary strings to win. If one of the strings involved bribery, or threats, or even killing a man, Tebo Rand was capable of pulling it the same as he would some other string that was perfectly honest.

Several years before he had been riding across Eastern Oregon and had stayed overnight at the Cross Heart. He had fallen in love with the outfit then, the spacious ranch house, the vast hay meadows, the open range that seemed to have no limit, and he had inquired about buying it.

At the time another company had owned the Cascade and Snake River Wagon Road Grant and had had great plans to develop it, but the panic had come along and the company had been forced to sell to a St. Louis group that included George Mandell. Rand had forgotten about the Cross Heart until this spring when he'd run into a man in a little town in western Kansas who was selling tickets for the drawing that was taking place now.

He bought one ticket, took the train to St. Louis, and went at once to the office of the company. As soon as he learned that Chauncey Ryan was hired to run the drawing in Oregon, he looked the man up. He always operated on the principle that any man had a price. He had to go to $10,000 before he reached Ryan's price.

After that it had been simply a matter of working out the details. He took a train to California, bought a team, wagon, and camping outfit in Alturas, and drove north to Mallard Lake, being one of the first to arrive at the so-called townsite.

At first he had been satisfied with the arrangement. He had watched the people come in and make camp; he had seen the sprawling tent city come into existence with its saloons and brothels and gambling places. He had seen Chauncey Ryan and Babs arrive with George Mandell and take over the old ranch house. He had seen young Johnny Lund ride in from Piute, the county seat, and do a good job keeping order. Then the whole scheme had started to go sour.

Men who had not been in this country did not realize how barren most of it was and how little could be done with ten acres. Many of them who had bought tickets thought that by buying ten, they would have a single piece of land that was one hundred acres in size. Now they discovered that they would, in all probability, end up with ten small pieces scattered from one end of the wagon road grant to the other.

Rand had not realized, and he was reasonably sure that George Mandell and the other owners had not realized, the enormity of the lies told by the ticket salesmen. Now that the men, and in many cases their families, were actually here on the ground, they saw how completely they had been bilked and their anger had been soaring ever since.

It was true that some of the men had ridden to the Cross Heart and had looked at it and been impressed. Others had seen the tracts of valuable timber and the few larger pieces of land that could be irrigated and had been equally impressed.

Even so, they were aware that only one of them would draw the Cross Heart. Only a few others, perhaps no more than a dozen, would draw a piece of timber land or a potential irrigated farm.

When they took time to figure the odds against them, the fury spread like a contagious fever.

Someone, and Rand still did not know who or why, started the story that the whole deal had been rigged from the first and Ryan, or Ryan and Mandell together, had conspired to keep the Cross Heart and the best of the timber and irrigated land. Of course no one suspected Rand because he was just one of the suckers who had bought a ticket, but if this fury exploded into action, the damage would be done and Rand's scheme would go down the drain if Ryan was murdered.

After Al Dillon's attempt to shoot Ryan had failed, Tebo Rand returned to his wagon, built up his fire and heated what was left of the supper coffee. He stared thoughtfully at the flames as he drank his coffee. He considered several questions. Why had Al Dillon of all people tried to shoot Ryan? Who else, if anybody, was involved? How could he stop the thing?

He had no answers. Several men and their wives paused at his fire to talk, all of them bitter toward Ryan and all believing the rumor that he was a crook and the draw was not a fair one. Nothing that Rand could say changed their minds. He told them the same thing Ryan had, that if Chauncey Ryan was shot or scared off the job, the drawing would be delayed for weeks.

It didn't make any difference. The righteous

anger of these people who had come hundreds and in some cases thousands of miles and then learned they had bought a pig in a poke was so great that it would take very little to make them kill and burn and end up destroying any chance Tebo Rand had of getting the Cross Heart.

One man Rand knew by name, Norman Bradford, stopped and said grimly, "I never in my life had any part in killing a human being, but if somebody gives the word, I'll be the first to put a rope on Chauncey Ryan's neck."

"And then hang for murder yourself?" Rand asked.

"They can't hang all of us," Bradford snapped. "There must be five hundred of us here. Maybe more. Before the week's out somebody is gonna say let's go get the bastard and by God, I'll be right behind him."

"Why not wait till after the Cross Heart is drawn?" Rand asked. "You might get it. Or me. Or one of your neighbors."

Bradford looked Rand in the eyes. He said, "It won't be me who gets it. If it's you or one of my neighbors, I'll figure you or him are in cahoots with Chauncey Ryan. Come on, Martha."

He stalked off into the darkness, his wife beside him. So it went. Even after everyone had gone to his wagon, Rand could still hear the sullen rumble of talk. Finally the rumble died, but Rand's nerves did not relax.

He had been all over the West, he had seen men lynched, and he knew the symptoms of the fever. It was a feeling in the air, the same kind of feeling that comes in the breathless stillness just before an electric storm strikes with its devastating power.

A lynching was understandable, but Al Dillon's effort to shoot Ryan wasn't. Dillon simply wasn't that kind of man. When Rand's thoughts came to a blank wall and he could stand it no longer, he kicked out his fire and went to Dillon's camp. He had visited with Dillon several times and was attracted by his daughter Ann.

She was only about twenty and he was forty-five, but he was not willing to concede that age made any difference. He had not told her he liked her, but he had gone out of his way to be friendly and had spent a good deal of time with her, so he had a notion she understood his feelings.

He knew the hour was late, but he didn't stop on that account. When he reached the Dillon wagon and saw that a lantern was still lighted, he knew she was awake.

He straddled the tongue and, with his head close to the opening in the canvas, called, "Ann! You awake?"

There was silence for a moment before she asked, "Who is it?"

"Tebo Rand. I want to talk to you."

"It's late and I'm getting ready for bed."

"I know it's late," he said impatiently, "but it's important. I don't want to wait until morning."

Again there was silence, then she said, "I'm here." In the starlight he saw her face in the opening.

"You know about your father?"

"Yes," the girl answered. "I talked to him a while ago."

"Did he tell you anything about why he did it?" Rand asked. "Or where he got the gun? He told me the other day he didn't own a gun and it took every cent he could raise to buy one ticket and enough grub to get here."

She didn't answer for a time. He said, "Listen, Ann. I haven't told you, but you must know that I'm very fond of you. I'm not a poor man. If I don't get a good piece of land in the draw, I won't be hurt. You're going to need someone to look out for you, now that Al's in jail, and I want to do it."

"You are very kind, Mr. Rand," she said, "but I can still look out for myself. Pa didn't tell me much we didn't already know. You are right that he didn't own a gun and he wouldn't tell me who gave it to him. He did say that several men want Ryan and Mandell murdered. They think the company will send new men who will give them an honest draw."

"Who are they, Ann?" Rand demanded. "Did

he name the men who want Ryan and Mandell murdered?"

"No, he wouldn't name them," she said. "Now if you'll excuse me, I'll go to bed."

Her head disappeared. A moment later she blew the lantern out. Rand stood there for a time, as uncertain about what he should do as he had been before he came. Something had been responsible for the rumor that the draw was crooked, but he didn't know what it was. Until he found out who had started it, he was not likely to find out why.

He walked back to his wagon, then on a sudden impulse, he turned and worked his way toward the road. He hadn't spoken to Ryan since the man had arrived, but he decided he'd better see him, although he was very much aware that he had to be careful. If they were seen talking together, it could add fuel to the fire and get him lynched along with Chauncey Ryan and George Mandell.

When he reached the ranch house, he circled around to the back and stood there wondering how he could attract Ryan's attention without getting into the light and being seen by anyone who might be watching. He had no idea whether other settlers were out there in the darkness or not, but he could not afford to run the risk.

He moved forward, hugging the wall, and stopped before he reached the first lighted window. The window was open and he heard the talk between Ryan and Mandell, and Mandell's statement that he was going to wire for the sheriff to come. That was fine. Johnny Lund was a good deputy and he had the guts to do the job, but he was young and inexperienced. The mere presence of the sheriff would go a long ways toward quieting the growing threat of violence.

He listened to the conversation between Ryan and Babs, wondering if he could call Ryan out of the house without arousing the suspicion of anyone who might be watching. Then he realized that Babs was leaving to talk to Johnny Lund, so he slid back to the rear corner and waited. A moment later Babs rounded the front corner and walked along the side of the house toward him.

He said softly, "It's Tebo Rand, Babs. Don't do anything to give me away. Keep coming just the way you were."

She jumped and started to turn back, then thought better of it and continued walking toward him. When she reached him, she said, "You are a damned fool. All one of these suspicious suckers need is to see you coming here and we'll all swing from a limb."

"I know it," he said impatiently. "That's why I've stayed in the dark. I want you to go back and tell Ryan to come here. He's the one I want to talk to. Blow the lamp out so nobody will see him leave."

She hesitated, then she said, "I still think you're

a fool. We're all sitting on the anxious seat and we can't afford a slip."

But she turned without further argument and walked back the way she had come. A moment later the lamp went out and presently Rand heard Chauncey Ryan's steps and saw his tall figure in the starlight.

"I'm back here," Rand said in a low voice.

Ryan stopped a few feet from him. "Babs is right. You're a fool for risking this."

"All right, I'm a fool," Rand said testily, "but I wouldn't have come if I hadn't thought it was important. First, I'm out there among the suckers. I'm one of them. I hear them talk. I know what they're thinking and how they feel. Do you?"

"I've got a pretty good idea," Ryan said, "but go ahead. Tell me."

"They're sore," Rand said. "They're so damned sore that they're talking about lynching you and Mandell. It's not just that they think they were bilked when they bought the tickets. They're convinced they won't get an honest draw, and they think they might if the company sends new men. All right, that raises the second point. Why do they believe the draw won't be honest?"

"I don't know," Ryan answered hotly. "You don't think I've told anything? Or Babs?"

"I wonder," Rand said softly. "If I knew for sure that you'd taken a drink too many and made a slip, I'd kill you right where you stand."

"I haven't," Ryan said. "Neither has Babs. If you came here to ask me that . . ."

"No, I had a better reason for coming," Rand said. "I know this Al Dillon who tried to shoot you tonight. He's a nothing. He doesn't even own a gun. I haven't been able to find out who gave him the gun or what set him off, but I know there are other men involved. It's a sure bet they'll either try to gun you down during one of the drawings or work up a lynch mob."

He could almost smell the fear that his words aroused in Chauncey Ryan. He heard the man's labored breathing, then his hoarse voice, "You make a man feel real good."

"I thought you'd better know and you'd better tell Mandell," Rand said. "I've got too much invested in you to lose out now. You tell Mandell to get Plug Tully and his gunslicks to guard the house and to circulate through the crowd while the drawing's going on. I'll go to the deputy or the sheriff when he gets here if I find out who the men are that worked Dillon up enough to shoot at you."

He slipped back and made another circle through the sagebrush as he returned to his wagon. All the time the same thought continued to nag him. There had to be something that had started the rumor about the crooked draw, but still he had no answer.

CHAPTER V

Johnny Lund woke suddenly, feeling that someone was in the tent with him. For a few seconds he didn't move. His eyes were open, but he could not see anyone from his position. He slid his right hand away from his body, fingers searching for his gun that he knew was there somewhere on the ground not far away. He found it and, gripping the walnut butt, sat up suddenly and swung the barrel toward the front of the tent.

"Are you awake, Johnny?"

It was a woman's voice. He saw her then, crouched in the opening at the front of the tent. He demanded, "Who is it?"

"Babs Ryan. I want to talk to you."

"My God," he whispered. "Do you know how close I came to shooting you? Don't do things like that."

"I guess I didn't think of that possibility," she admitted as she came on into the tent and sat down beside him. "I was afraid you were asleep and might be grumpy about me waking you up."

"I am," he said. "I'm a bear. Now what the devil do you want?"

"I want to talk. It's kind of lonesome in the house with just Dad. George Mandell isn't there very much. He isn't what you'd call good company anyhow. He spends most of his time in one of the saloons or those . . . those tents at the other end of Main Street."

Johnny knew how George Mandell spent his time. He had thought from the first that it was a poor kind of land company that couldn't send a better man than Mandell to represent it or a higher caliber of guards than Plug Tully's outfit, if guards were necessary. When it came right down to it, he didn't think much of Chauncey Ryan, either. Babs seemed to be the only decent one in the bunch.

He laid the gun down beside him. "Seems to me you could find a better time to come to talk than the middle of the night."

"Well, you are grumpy." She sighed. "I hoped you'd be in a good mood. You know, Johnny, I don't get much chance to see you in the daytime. You're on the prowl all the time looking for trouble so you can stop it, and I sleep late in the morning. I'm up late helping Dad with the paper work. Besides, I like to stay up at night and sleep till noon." She giggled. "That's what the mornings are for, Johnny."

Her face was a faint blob in the darkness. She was sitting very close to him and leaning forward so her face almost touched his. He found himself breathing hard. He had to tell himself she was just a child, that she didn't know what she was doing.

He realized at once he was lying to himself. She knew exactly what she was doing, showing the kind of inherent wisdom that every woman has when she's born. Babs was one who would use it.

He eased a little farther away from her. "Let's talk about what you came to talk about and then you go back to the house and let me sleep."

"I can't sleep," she said. "I've been in bed and all I did was to toss and turn. I thought about you and I wanted to talk. I knew you'd be lonesome out here by yourself."

"Lonesome when I'm sound asleep? Listen, if you don't have something to talk about . . ."

"Oh, I have something to talk about, all right," she broke in. "Did you ever get shot at?"

"Not exactly," he admitted. "Not the way your pa was tonight."

"I guess we haven't really thanked you for saving our lives," she said. "That's what it amounted to. If you hadn't taken care of Dillon he'd have kept on shooting until he killed Dad. Then he'd have shot me, too. I was scared, Johnny. I'm still scared." She fell against him and began to cry. "Hold me, Johnny. Hold me tight so I won't be afraid."

He put an arm around her and she flung both arms around him and hugged him. He didn't know what to do with her, and suddenly he realized that if Chauncey Ryan came looking for her and found her here in his tent and in his arms, there'd be hell to pay.

"You can't stay here," he said. "You go on back to your room. Your pa wouldn't like it if he found you with me."

"Wouldn't like it?" she whispered. "Johnny, you don't know him. He'd like it just fine. He doesn't care about anything but his old drawing." Her lips slid along his cheek and searched for his mouth. "I just want to be held and comforted a little and then I'll go back to my own bed."

"You go right now." He pushed her away. "You're a child and I don't want to be responsible . . ."

"Child?" She began to cry again. Finally she managed to say, "I like that, being called a child. I'm a lot older than you think. I'm old enough to know what I want. I like you and I've never had a chance to tell you before."

How had he ever got into a situation like this? he asked himself. Maybe she was right about being older than he thought. He had the feeling again that she knew exactly what she was doing, that she had the wisdom of Eve. He guessed he was as naive and ignorant as he had thought she was.

She was sobbing one minute as if her heart was broken, then she was all over him the next, kissing him and whispering, "I just wanted to tell you how grateful I am for saving my life and I wanted to tell you how brave I thought you were. I don't think Plug Tully's men are going to be one bit of help."

He felt the pressure of her strong, young breasts against him, he tasted the sweetness of her lips and for a moment he held her in his arms and returned her kiss. For some reason a warning began nagging him. He wished it hadn't come, but it was there. He couldn't define it. Maybe it was the fear that Chauncey Ryan would poke his head into the tent any minute. If Ryan went to Sheriff Ed Neal about it, Johnny would be in trouble. Ryan might even blackmail him.

Once more he pushed her back and slid away from her so that he was in the front of the tent. He said, "Babs, this is very pleasant and I think you are a sweet girl, but this is all. Vamoose."

She sighed. "I thought it was pleasant, too. Maybe you're not as much of a man as I thought you were. I guess George Mandell was right to send for the sheriff."

"What?"

"You heard what I said." She laughed softly. "I thought that would make you change your tune. He talked it over with Dad. They said you were young and inexperienced, so Mandell went to the telegraph office and wired the sheriff to come."

Johnny groaned. "I've taken care of things so far, haven't I? What does that fool Mandell want? I'm going to tell him . . ."

"Oh, no," she whispered. "Don't tell him anything. He'd be mad if he knew I was here and talking to you and all. He thinks you handled everything fine and dandy. So does Dad. But there are so many of these people and we keep hearing talk about a conspiracy to kill Dad and Mandell. Maybe me, too. You stopped Dillon tonight, but somebody else might try it. Or there might be a terrible riot if these crazy people keep talking about the drawing being crooked."

"I'll break Mandell's neck," Johnny said angrily. "Ed Neal will fire me when he gets here."

"Oh, no he won't," she said. "I'll talk to him. Dad will talk to him, too. But we're awfully scared, Johnny. Is there someone else . . . well, are there a lot of men in this with Dillon? Did he tell you anything when you arrested him?"

"No. I guess there are some other men with him, but he didn't tell me anything. We've just got to keep our eyes open."

"I don't know if I want to get back on that platform or not," she said. "Well, I'm going to bed and let you sleep, Johnny. I apologize for being so bold, but I was frightened." She slipped out of the tent, whispered, "Good night," and was gone.

He hunkered there for a long time in the opening under the tent flap that had been turned back. He rolled and fired a cigarette, smoked it, and flipped the stub into the sagebrush. Something hadn't been quite right. She'd acted like a hysterical girl, throwing herself at him the way she had. He wondered how far she would have gone if he'd responded.

Now, thinking about it, he had an idea that was upsetting. Maybe she hadn't come to be comforted and to thank him at all. Maybe she had intended to quiz him about the shooting, hoping he would tell her who had been involved with Al Dillon. Then she would tell Ryan and Ryan would tell Plug Tully and whoever he named would turn up missing.

He retrieved his gun and started to walk, knowing he could not sleep any more tonight. This was a hell of a situation, he told himself. He wanted to make good on his job, wanted it more than anything else in the world. So far he had done all right, and Mandell had no grounds to send for Ed Neal.

He walked the length of Main Street. The lights were out. For the moment there was no sound except the barking of a dog from somewhere over toward the lake. A rooster crowed, then another. He passed the saloons and the brothels at the end of the street, pausing as he wondered if Ed Neal would expect him to close them. Ed hadn't said so.

As long as they weren't creating a disturbance, he couldn't see any reason to close them. They served a purpose for some men, and perhaps helped protect girls like Babs. Then, remembering how she had kissed him, he had a guilty thought. Perhaps she was no better than the girls in these tents. He turned back, wondering how old she was. One thing was sure. She was not the innocent sixteen-year-old girl she publicly pretended to be.

He heard someone chopping wood back of Ma Ketchum's Kitchen. When he reached it, he saw that she had lighted a lamp and had started coffee. He might just as well have breakfast.

Dawn was beginning to show above the distant rimrock to the east. As he turned into the big tent, he told himself he was going to find out what Al Dillon knew about this so-called conspiracy. The man was stupid and a coward, but somebody had given him the gun he'd used and Johnny was going to find out who that somebody was if he had to beat Dillon half to death.

CHAPTER VI

Ma Ketchum's Kitchen was a big tent with a range and work table and shelves for sacks and cans of food in the center. This area was surrounded by a counter which was made up of rough pine boards laid across sawhorses. Additional boards on short-legged sawhorses served as seats.

Johnny had known Ma Ketchum for years. She'd had a cafe in Piute as long as he could remember. She was an ample-breasted woman with red hair and a temper to match, but she was good hearted and usually she'd had plenty of excuse when she'd blown up at somebody.

When Ma heard about the drawing and the new town of Mallard City, she locked up her cafe in Piute, hired a young man named Billy Bean who had gone through school with Johnny, and bought two teams and wagons. She loaded one with grub and the other with her kitchen equipment, and started south.

Arriving with the first settlers and businessmen, she had set up her tent and was in business in less than twenty-four hours. As she'd told Johnny with considerable pride, she'd had a land office business ever since. The only trouble was she was lucky to get four or five hours sleep a night. Billy helped her wait on the customers, but she needed a girl and so far she hadn't found one she wanted to hire.

She was slicing bacon when Johnny came in. She looked up and nodded. "Good morning, Johnny. How's our tough, gunslinger deputy today?"

"Fine," Johnny said, "except that I don't feel so tough. Looks like I'd better practice up on gunslinging after what happened last night."

"It sure does," Ma agreed. "How come you're up so early this morning?"

"I had trouble sleeping," he answered. "Ain't that coffee done yet?"

"Oh, it won't take the hair off your chest yet," Ma said, "but it's drinkable. What'll you have this morning?"

"Flapjacks, bacon, and more coffee," Johnny said.

Ma poured his coffee, then dropped bacon into a frying pan and set it on the stove. She stirred the flapjack dough with gusto, then paused to ask, "What do you make of it? That shooting last night?"

"Trouble," Johnny answered. "Big trouble. This Al Dillon who did the shooting don't amount to nothing. That's the part I don't savvy. What possessed him to try to shoot Ryan is more'n I know."

Ma spooned three dips of flapjack dough into a frying pan. "Who knows what gets into a man's head when he's desperate enough? Or what it'll make him do? I can tell you one thing, from the talk I hear. Right now there's five hundred or more men camped around here or staying in the hotels, and they're all about as desperate as they can get."

She stood facing the stove, her back to Johnny, until the bacon and flapjacks were done, then she lifted them from the frying pan to a plate and set it in front of Johnny. Billy Bean came in through the back of the tent and dropped an armload of wood beside the stove.

Bean nodded at Johnny and said, "Good morning, Deputy."

Johnny said between mouthfuls, "Good morning, Billy. If I remember it, you used to be a pretty good hand with a gun. How about helping me out if this pot boils over? I sure can't count on Plug Tully and his hardcases."

"Not me," Billy said. "Taking the star from Ed Neal was your idea. Working for Ma was mine."

He wheeled and strode out of the tent. A moment later Johnny heard his ax as he attacked the woodpile again. Ma sighed. "Well, I guess you can't really blame him, Johnny."

The sun was up now, daylight streaming in through the tent door. Ma blew the lamp out and added slowly, "I usually know enough to keep my big mouth shut, but I'm going to give you some advice anyhow. Send for Ed Neal. This is going to take more'n one man. It's written in the book."

Johnny shook his head. "I won't send for him, Ma. When he sent me down here, he said this was my show." He took a drink of coffee, wondering if he was being too stubborn about it. But it wasn't just a matter of stubbornness. Neal had made it plain and no event could change what he had said. "Fix up a bait of breakfast for my prisoner. I'll take it to him as soon as I finish eating."

When Ma handed him a plate and tin cup of coffee a few minutes later, he said, "Al Dillon has a grown daughter named Ann. She's going to need help, now I've got her pa locked up. Think you could use her?"

"I might if she's the right kind of girl," Ma said, "though from what I've heard of Al Dillon, I don't see how his daughter could be the right kind."

"She is," Johnny said. "She must have had a good mother. She sure didn't take after her pa."

"You sweet on her?" Ma asked.

"I might be," Johnny admitted. "She's the kind of girl I've been looking for."

"Bring her around," Ma said. "I'll have a look at her."

"I'll have her here before noon," Johnny said, and left the tent.

He walked to the jail, the morning sunlight

golden bright, a faint dew still on the grass at the edges of the street sparkling like countless tiny diamonds. Later in the day there would be a brittleness in the air, and the smell of sage, and unless a wind came up, the dust raised by men and horses would cling to the earth and irritate people's nostrils and throats and hone tempers that were already sharp to an even finer edge.

The camp was beginning to come to life. Johnny heard children yelling at each other and laughing, and mothers calling them to breakfast. Smoke from cook fires drifted toward him. A man coughed, and from somewhere among the wagons to his left a dog fight broke out with a great deal of yelping. A man bellowed, "Let 'em fight it out, damn it. That cur of yours has been asking for a beating ever since you got here."

Even dogs had their troubles, Johnny thought as he unlocked the jail door and pulled it open. He had set the plate and cup on the ground. Now he picked them up, calling, "Dillon, here's your breakfast."

The man shambled toward him from the dark interior of the building, blinking in the sunlight. He said, "Mind if I eat outside? Makes a man realize how important the sun is when you're stuck in a hole like this."

"Right here by the door," Johnny said. "You get up and make a run for it and you're a dead man."

Dillon hunkered beside the door, looking at

Johnny resentfully. "I ain't figgering on making no run for it," he said. "I'm lucky to be alive. I figure on you keeping me alive, now that I'm your prisoner."

He started to eat wolfishly as if he hadn't had a meal for days. Perhaps he hadn't, Johnny thought, and then he remembered Ann and wondered when she had eaten. He should have thought about her working for Ma before this, but he hadn't been concerned as long as Dillon had been free. Not that it made much difference, with Dillon being as completely no good as he was. Still, it had been the man's responsibility to support Ann, and his fault if they starved.

Johnny rolled and lighted a cigarette, then he said, "Just why do you think I'll have a problem keeping you alive, Dillon?"

Dillon had started to drink his coffee. Johnny's question upset him. He choked and set his tin cup on the ground beside him. He wiped his mouth on his sleeve and shook his head, eyeing Johnny warily. "No good reason," he said. "I just figgered somebody might come along and poke a gun through one of them windows and let me have it."

"Why?" Johnny asked. "That's what I'm trying to get out of you. What reason would any man have for killing you?"

Dillon picked up his cup and started sipping his coffee again. He had no intention of answering,

Johnny saw, so he said, "Dillon, I wouldn't be above taking you inside the jail and pulling the door shut and beating you half to death if you don't tell me what I want to know. I might even take my knife and carve you up some if you don't talk."

Dillon began to shake. He set the empty cup down and started edging away from Johnny. Johnny patted the butt of his gun. "Remember what I said. You make a run for it and you're dead. Now I asked you a question. If I get an honest answer, I won't touch you, but if you don't answer, or if you lie to me, you're going to wish you had never been born."

"What was the question?" Dillon asked.

"I'll come at it another way," Johnny said. "You didn't own a gun. Somebody gave you one and talked you into trying to murder Ryan. Who was it?"

For a long time Dillon stared at the ground in front of him. Johnny pulled his knife out of his pocket and opened the big blade. He made a show out of testing the edge, then he began whetting it on the side of one of his boots.

Finally Dillon mumbled, "That's why I figure you'd better protect me. If I tell you who gave me the gun, you'll go see him and tell him what I told you and then he'll come and try to kill me."

"You should have thought of that when you took the gun," Johnny said. "I'm running low on patience, and when I run clean out, you'n me are going inside the jail. All the yelling you can do won't help you none."

Johnny tested the edge of the blade again, then leaned forward, his gaze on Dillon's white face. "Which ear do you want to lose first?" He paused, and then added, "Now that I think about it, I guess I'll take both of 'em."

"You're bulling me," Dillon said hoarsely, "but I'll tell you. It was Chuck O'Leary. His wagon is next to mine. You know him?"

Johnny shook his head. "No."

"Well, we talked about it several times," Dillon went on. "He's dead sure it's a crooked draw. The one chance any of us have to get rich on this deal is to get the Cross Heart. I've wanted to do something for Ann ever since she was born. This is the only opportunity I ever had, so I took all the money we had and bought one ticket. When they pulled my number last night and then told me I had nothing, I seen the one big chance I had go down the drain. I went kind of crazy, I guess. That's why I used O'Leary's gun."

"There's talk about a plot," Johnny said. "Of a bunch of men working out a scheme to murder Ryan. Who are the others beside you and O'Leary?"

"I dunno and that's the truth," Dillon said. "You can carve me up like a Thanksgiving turkey or beat me to death, but I can't tell you something

I don't know. There is some kind of a plot. I guess about half a dozen men are in it. The only name I ever heard except O'Leary's is Norman Bradford."

Johnny studied him a moment, thinking this was probably the truth. Well, he had enough to start with. He saw Dillon's hand go up to his shirt pocket and then fall away as if only then realizing he didn't have the makings. Johnny tossed him a sack of Bull Durham and some papers to him. He dug several matches out of his pocket and gave them to Dillon.

"Keep 'em," Johnny said.

"Thank you," Dillon said gratefully. "Been a while since I've had a smoke."

Johnny jabbed a thumb at the door. "Inside, Dillon. I can't stay here all the time to guard you, but I don't think anybody is gonna get high enough to shoot through one of those windows. He couldn't do it without a ladder anyhow. I'll have a talk with O'Leary and I'll tell him that if anything happens to you, he's the first one I'll look for."

Dillon got up and gazed along the street as if he were half dazed. Johnny guessed he was hoping to see O'Leary or someone coming to rescue him. A dozen or more men were gathered in little knots talking earnestly about something, probably the crooked draw that seemed to be on everybody's tongue these days.

No one was paying any attention to Dillon. Probably the men who were in the street didn't even know who he was. He sighed and stepped through the door and back into the near darkness of the jail. Johnny pulled the door shut and locked it, then picked up the cup and plate and took them back to Ma's Kitchen.

He had heard of men being behind the door when the Lord passed out the brains. He guessed that was where Dillon was standing when the guts were being handed out. Al Dillon had certainly come up missing as far as plain, cold courage was concerned.

CHAPTER VII

Tebo Rand woke before dawn and lay on his back under his wagon, feeling short of sleep, but unable to drop off again. He'd had such a good scheme, he had thought, foolproof because he was paying Chauncey Ryan and Babs enough for them to deliver what they had promised. Once they had done what he was paying them for, they'd have to keep their mouths shut.

He'd pretended to be one of the settlers; he'd echoed their complaints and threats, but all the time he had his own interests. The settlers could blame the company or Ryan for a crooked draw, but they would never dream of blaming one of their own.

The danger right now was that Ryan might be murdered by the mob before he could keep his agreement. That brought Rand back to the question that had made him uneasy last night. Now, in this last hour before dawn, it was what was keeping him awake. Why and how had this rumor about a crooked draw ever got started?

The early morning light moved in across the flat, the eastern sky flaming with the sunrise. No use staying here, Rand thought, so he rolled out from under the wagon, tossed his blankets inside, and poured water from his bucket into a wash pan.

He sloshed water on his face, shivering a little because the water was cold and the air held the cold bite of the frosty night. It would be another hour or two before the sun cut away the chill.

He picked up the coffee pot and then suddenly it occurred to him that Ann Dillon might not have anything to eat in her wagon. He knew that she and her father had had very little to eat in the past three days. He wanted Ann. He wanted her very much, and with her father gone, she would be frightened and hungry. Her physical needs along with the fact that she was alone in a big crowd of people, most of them rough men, should be enough to make it easy to bend her to his will.

This was probably the best opportunity he would ever have, he thought, so he had better take advantage of it. He carried a coffee pot and a sack of coffee to the Dillon wagon. There was no wood for a cook fire, so he returned to his wagon for an armload of wood. He built a fire, making no effort to be quiet because it was time for Ann to get up.

He went back to his wagon for bacon and eggs. When he returned to the Dillon camp, his fire was burning well. He opened the Dillon grub box and took out a frying pan, then sliced bacon into it and set it on the fire.

"Ann, you awake?" he called.

She looked out at him. “I’m awake, but I don’t know why. There’s nothing for me to do today. I might just as well keep on sleeping.”

“Oh, no, don’t go back to bed,” he said. “I’ll have breakfast ready for you in a minute. I don’t like to eat alone. How about joining me?”

She hesitated, looking at him with distaste. He was irritated, but he had to remember she was less than half his age. He was going to have to move slowly and carefully so he would not offend her, he thought. She would naturally prefer some young buck like that squirt of a deputy, but Johnny Lund couldn’t do anything for her, and Tebo Rand could do a great deal. It was time she knew. If she didn’t, he’d better tell her.

“All right,” she said. “Give me five minutes.”

He opened her grub box again and took out tin cups. By the time she stepped out of the wagon, he had finished frying the bacon and had broken half a dozen eggs into the grease. He motioned for her to sit down and nodded approvingly. He said, “You’re mighty pretty this morning, Ann.”

He wasn’t lying to her. She was wearing a clean pink dress and had brushed and pinned up her auburn hair. He added, “I thought you might like some eggs for breakfast. I brought these up from Alturas. I don’t suppose you’ve had any lately. The damned tent stores charge you twice what anything’s worth.”

She flushed and bit her lip for a moment before

she said anything. Finally she nodded. "No, I haven't had an egg for a long time."

He didn't say anything more until the eggs were cooked. He divided them between the two plates, poured the coffee, and handed her a plate and cup. She ate hungrily, and he decided she would have gone hungry this morning if he hadn't fixed breakfast for her.

"Have you seen your pa since he was arrested?" Rand asked between mouthfuls of egg.

"I saw him last night," she said. "I told you that when you came to the wagon."

"Yes, so you did," Rand said. "What do you suppose that fool deputy is going to do with him?"

"He's not a fool deputy," she said hotly. "He's been very kind to me. It was Pa who acted like a fool and Johnny Lund had to arrest him."

"He done a fool thing and that's a fact," Rand agreed.

He didn't ask the question a second time. It was plain that Ann had a soft spot in her heart for Lund and Rand would only make the situation worse by condemning him. So they finished eating and were on their second cup of coffee when Rand asked, "Have you seen the Cross Heart?"

She shook her head. "Neither has Pa, but we've heard so much about it that it seems like we've seen it."

"It's a good spread," he said. "I'm going to get it in one way or the other. I told you it didn't make any difference whether I drew a good piece of land or not. I'm probably the only man in camp who has plenty of money. If I don't get the Cross Heart on the draw, I'll buy it from whoever does get it. I expect to draw it, though. I've bought several tickets, so percentage-wise my chances should be good."

"Most men are like Pa," she said. "If they draw it, they'll figure on operating it."

"It wouldn't be possible for most of the men who are camped here to run it," he said. "It takes a lot of money to operate a spread as big as the Cross Heart, and I doubt if ten men in the whole crowd have that kind of money." He gave her a sharp glance, and added, "I have."

She didn't say anything. She didn't even look at him, but stared at the fire. He set his coffee cup on the ground and edged closer to her. He said, "Ann, I'm a single man. I told you last night I was fond of you, but I guess you knew that." He hesitated, then decided he'd go all the way, now that he'd started. "I would like to have a wife who could enjoy living on the Cross Heart with me. It would mean some hard work, but I expect you've been used to hard work all your life."

He stopped, looking at the profile of her face. Still she didn't say a word or look at him. He asked, "Ann, will you marry me?"

She got to her feet. He rose, too, and faced her. She wasn't laughing at him exactly, but she was amused. She said, "I'm sorry, Mr. Rand, but I'm afraid I'm too young for you. I haven't had my twentieth birthday."

Anger boiled up in him, but he kept it bottled up. He said, "Lots of men my age marry women your age. I've got a great deal to offer you. Besides, with your pa in jail, you need someone to take care of you."

"I told you before I can take care of myself," she said. "As a matter of fact, I've taken care of myself most of my life. My mother died when I was twelve. Pa has never been a man to earn a living for himself, let alone a daughter, so I've had to work for other people just to stay alive."

"How can you take care of yourself in a place like this?" he demanded. "You haven't got anything to eat in your wagon and these tent stores won't give any credit. You can't get work and you're three days travel from the nearest town. You'll starve to death."

She did look at him now, her eyes narrowed and filled with anger. "Are you trying to take advantage of my situation to make me marry you? It won't work, Mr. Rand. I'll starve before I let a man force me into marriage, especially one I don't love, and I certainly don't love you."

This was too much. Now that he had come this far and had offered her marriage, he could not accept defeat. He gripped her shoulders. "You listen to me," he said. "I'm not trying to take advantage of you. I offered you marriage. What else can a man offer?"

"Nothing," she answered, "but you see, I've never asked anything from you. I just don't want to marry you. Now will you please let me go? You're hurting me."

He shook her, tightening his grip instead of letting her go. He said, "I'm used to getting what I want and I want to marry you. I'll even see the deputy about letting your pa go. He's not worth a damn, but I'll give him work or just a place to live if he don't want to work. You're not in position to say no to me. Was I right about you being out of grub?"

"Yes."

"All right then, damn it." He shook her again to emphasize what he was saying. "You didn't even have any wood for a fire when I came over here. Now you'd better change your tune in a hurry. I'm offering you a life of comfort and security. I'm going to have the Cross Heart. It can be your home if you'll take it. It's . . ."

He stopped. He was being a fool and that was no way to win the girl, but now, looking at her set, angry face, he didn't know what to say or do. He couldn't keep on begging her. He just stood there, looking at her and holding her shoulders in that tight grip, and all the time he was searching his mind for something he could say that would change her mind.

She tried to jerk free, but she could not. She couldn't lift her hand to slap his face, so she did the only thing she could. She kicked him hard just above the top of his left boot, cracking him on the shin. He let out a yelp of pain and released his grip. His reaction was instinctive. He slapped her face, staggering her.

The next thing Rand knew a strong hand had him by an arm and he was being jerked around. A fist slammed against his jaw and he sprawled full length on the ground beside the fire. He blinked and looked up into the grim face of Johnny Lund.

"Get on your feet, bucko," Johnny said. "You're good at hitting a woman. Now try hitting a man."

CHAPTER VIII

For a moment Tebo Rand lay staring up at Johnny, shocked and dazed. He was unable, Johnny thought, to believe what had happened. Then, slowly, he pulled himself to his knees. "I'm going to kill you," he said thickly, and came on up to his feet and rushed at Johnny.

Rand was a bigger and stronger man than Johnny, but he was more than twice Johnny's age, and age has a way of slowing a man down, a fact that Tebo Rand refused to recognize, and a fact that Johnny counted on. He waited until Rand was almost on him, a big fist swinging upward from his boot tops. Quickly Johnny wheeled to one side, clipped Rand on the side of the head and knocked him down again.

"All right," Johnny said. "I like the way you kill me. Try once more."

Rand shook his head and came slowly to his feet. He rushed Johnny again, a snarling, cursing animal, but this time Johnny didn't sidestep. He stood his ground, and at exactly the right second, took one step forward and sledged Rand on the mouth with a hard right. The blow snapped his head back as it cut his lips and brought a stream of blood pouring down his chin.

For an instant Rand remained upright as if he

were suspended on an invisible string, a rag doll that was bent at knee and hip and wanted to go down, but could not. Johnny hit him again, this time squarely on the jaw, a powerful, upswinging left, and Rand was out cold when he hit the ground.

Johnny rubbed his bruised knuckles on his pants legs as he turned to the wide-eyed girl. She whispered, "Why, Mr. Lund, he never touched you. Not once."

"My friends call me Johnny," he said. "I'd like to count you among them."

"Of course," she said, "and I'm Ann as I'm sure you know." She looked down at the motionless Rand and shook her head. "I'm sorry about him. He was good to Pa. Always friendly, but I suppose he didn't mean it. He was trying to get on my good side."

"What was he doing when I came up?" Johnny asked. "I saw that he had his hands on your shoulders and you were trying to break free and couldn't. Then all of a sudden he let go and yelped like he was hurt and then whapped you on the face."

"You didn't see what I did," she said. "He's a strong man and I guess my shoulders are black and blue where he had hold of me. I kicked him on the shin right above his boot." She pointed at her feet. "My boot toes are hard, and I guess I really must have hurt him."

"I don't know much about him," Johnny said. "I've seen him around the camp and that's all I know about him, except that he has a good outfit and he hasn't made any trouble before this. What was the argument about?"

"He wanted to marry me," she answered, "but he just couldn't take no for an answer. He tried to buy me, really. He's got lots of money, he said, and he seemed to be absolutely certain he would get the Cross Heart in the drawing. If he didn't, he was going to buy it."

"Now that's interesting," Johnny said thoughtfully, "along with all of this talk about a crooked draw. Did he say just why he was so certain he'd get the Cross Heart?"

"No, except that he'd bought several tickets, so he said he had a good chance percentage-wise." She shook her head, and repeated, "I'm sorry about him." She glanced at Johnny. "He really was trying to help me, I guess. He built the fire and cooked breakfast for me, and this is the way I respond."

"He hit you a pretty good lick," Johnny said. "Don't seem to me that's the proper way to win a loving wife."

"No, it isn't," she agreed, "but what he told me was true enough. He said I couldn't afford to turn him down. He'd give me comfort and security, and I'd starve if I didn't accept him. I will, I guess. I don't have a cent of money and nothing to eat. I expect to work, but there aren't any jobs here for me."

"That's what I was coming to see you about," Johnny said. "I had breakfast at Ma's Kitchen. I've known her for years. She comes from Piute, you know, and that's my home. I knew that with your pa in jail, you'd need a job and I asked Ma if she could use you."

"I'd need a job whether Pa was free or in jail," she said bitterly. "What did Ma say?"

"She didn't promise anything," Johnny answered, "but she said she'd look you over, so come along. I'll take you to see her."

Ann didn't move or say anything. Tebo Rand had come around. Now he sat up and wiped a hand across his battered face. He said, "Where'd you find that club you hit me with? I never seen it."

"I used my fist," Johnny said. "I didn't need a club. In your day you were probably a purty good barroom brawler, but I'm too fast for you, Rand. I guess maybe you've slowed up. You didn't kill me as you promised."

"Too fast, you say?" Rand got to his feet and leaned against the back wheel of the Dillon wagon, scowling at Johnny. "We'll see as to that. The next time I'll use my gun and we'll find out who's too fast for who."

"I'll tell you one thing," Johnny said. "You come around bothering Ann again, and I'll be the one to use my gun. From now on just let her alone."

"You're talking, but I sure can't hear you," Rand said, and walked away toward his wagon.

Johnny started after him, but Ann caught his arm. "No," she said. "Don't hurt him any more."

"He'll probably try to dry-gulch me," Johnny said angrily. "I won't be safe as long as he's alive."

"I don't think he'll do that," Ann said. "Anyhow, you can't just walk over there and kill him like he was a . . . a bug or something."

"No, toting a star is a handicap sometimes," Johnny said. He stepped away from her wagon and looked around. "Your pa identified Chuck O'Leary as the man who gave him the gun."

"I should have guessed that," she said, and pointed to the wagon next to her. "That's O'Leary's outfit, but I don't see him. He's probably had breakfast and left. Pa spent a lot of time with him, but he would never come here to talk. He always acted like he was sneaking around doing something he shouldn't, or something he didn't want me to know about. I never liked him and I was surprised that Pa did."

"I'll come back and try to find him," Johnny said. "Right now I want you to come with me to Ma's Kitchen. Did you ever work in a restaurant?"

"Lots of times," she answered. "It's usually the

only kind of honest or decent work I can get."

They walked toward Mallard City's Main Street, if it could be called a main street. The wagons were not drawn up in any kind of pattern, but all of them left enough room between them and their neighbors for any to move out if necessary. No one spoke to Johnny, although several nodded at Ann and said, "Good morning."

To them a deputy was the enemy, Johnny thought. All of the settlers considered him part of the company and they probably were not able to distinguish between a neutral lawman and Plug Tully's tough hands who were hired by the company.

A chill coursed down Johnny's spine. He had never been treated this way before, never been made to feel he was the enemy of honest men. He stared straight ahead, ignoring the settlers' scowls. He realized he was scared and he didn't like the feeling; he sensed the sullen anger that gripped these men more strongly than he had felt it before.

It would take very little to turn them on him if he did something like arresting Chuck O'Leary. It would take even less to turn the crowd into a screaming, bloodthirsty mob that would raid the company's headquarters and murder Chauncey Ryan and George Mandell. Babs, too, perhaps. He had not been a lawman very long, but it had been long enough to realize that the veneer covering a civilized man is very thin. Too, sometimes the distinction between a man and an animal is almost as thin.

When they reached the street, they turned south toward Ma's Kitchen. Babs Ryan, wearing a bright red dress, sat in a rocking chair on the porch of the headquarters building. When she saw Johnny, she waved and called, "Good morning, Mr. Deputy."

He said, "Good morning," and went on with Ann who glanced obliquely at him.

"I see that Miss Ryan is a friend of yours," Ann said.

He was uncomfortable and showed it by saying in a grumpy tone, "No, I wouldn't call her that."

"I'm sure she would call you her friend," Ann said. "It's not my business to give you any advice, but I have some I want to give you."

"Go ahead," he said. "I always listen to advice and seldom take it."

She smiled. "That's what I thought. All right, just listen then. The settlers don't trust either Chauncey Ryan or the girl. If you want the settlers to trust you, or even listen to you, you're going to have to avoid both Ryan and the girl."

"I aim to if I can," he said, "and I think your advice is first rate. I don't trust Ryan or the girl, either, but the company has a right to be protected from the settlers just like the settlers expect to be protected from Plug Tully's bunch, so it may be impossible to avoid them."

She shrugged, and said, "At least I told you."

"Thank you kindly," he said.

They walked in silence for a time, Johnny thinking glumly that he was caught in the middle with neither side trusting him. He was alone. Sure, he was camped here with five hundred men and a few women and children, but except for a handful like Ma Ketchum, he was alone.

A moment later he said, "Here we are. Smile pretty when Ma sees you. She thinks it's important for the customers."

They turned into the big tent. He glanced at Ann. She was smiling and he told himself she was as good as hired. Ma couldn't afford to turn down a girl as pretty as Ann Dillon.

CHAPTER IX

Ma's Kitchen was jammed. Every seat around the counter was taken and other men were standing behind the ones who were seated, all waiting impatiently for a place at the counter. Johnny guessed that these men had been up late last night in the brothels or the saloons, and since there was nothing to do this morning except go back to the brothels and saloons, they had slept late. Now they were hungry and all wanted their breakfast at the same time.

"Whew," Ann whispered. "I didn't suppose she had this much business."

"Right now she's probably wishing she didn't have so much," Johnny said. "Come on."

He led the way to the back of the tent. Ma was standing over the big range frying bacon and flapjacks and filling plates as fast as she could. Sweat ran down her cheeks and dribbled from the bottom of her chin. She swiped a sleeve across her face, but more sweat popped out immediately. She yelled at Billy Bean to fetch in more wood and hand this plate to that man yonder and slice up another side of bacon. She'd have a heart attack if she kept this up, Johnny thought.

"Ma, here's Ann Dillon," Johnny said. "She wants to work."

"She sure came to the right place," Ma said, turning her head and giving Ann a brief glance. She handed the girl an apron. "Get in here. Look the menu over. See what the prices are. Take their money as soon as you set their plates down. If they don't have any money, yank the plate back and chase 'em out of here. We don't feed no dead beats. There's a six-shooter under the counter. If a man tries anything funny, let him have it."

Ann was shocked. She glanced at Johnny, saying, "She's a wild woman."

Ma didn't stop for a minute. "That I am," she said. "You'll be one, too, before the day's out. Billy, we need more wood. Johnny, get to hell out of here and let this girl work."

Johnny was glad to leave the tent and get away from the smoke and smell of grease and frying food. He took a deep breath of fresh air and turned toward the jail, thinking that Dillon would want to know about Ann. He had no idea how willing the girl was, but Ma would get work out of her if anybody could. He didn't think Ann was lazy, but she was Al Dillon's daughter, and if laziness and futility could be inherited, the chances were she'd be both lazy and futile.

When he reached the jail, he saw Babs leave her rocking chair on the porch of the old ranch house where the company's offices were located and come toward him. He didn't want to talk to her, not after what had happened last night.

She wasn't the child he had taken her for or she pretended to be. Maybe she was in years. He hadn't made up his mind about that, but she certainly wasn't in experience. The truth was he was afraid of her.

He turned off the road to the jail, but he didn't unlock the door. He called, "Dillon."

"I'm still here," Dillon answered sourly. "You figure maybe I'd left?"

"No," Johnny said. "I stopped to tell you that Ann is working in Ma's Kitchen. You don't need to be concerned about her."

A long pause, then Dillon said grudgingly, "Thanks, Deputy."

Johnny turned from the jail to the road to find Babs waiting for him, smiling as if she were anticipating a visit with him. She said, "Good morning, Deputy. Are you still speaking to me?"

"Sure," he said coolly, and would have walked past her if she hadn't caught an arm.

"Wait," she said. "You're not in a hurry, are you?"

"Yes," he said. "I've got a lot of things to do."

"They can wait," she said. "It's your duty to get acquainted with the daughter of the company auctioneer."

He shook his head. "The sheriff is the one who gives me my duties, and that ain't among 'em."

"Well then, you owe it to yourself," she said. "Come over to the house and I'll make some lemonade. Where else could you get lemonade in this terrible place?"

"Nowhere, but I'm not thirsty."

"Another time, then," she said. "What I really stopped you for was to ask about my competition."

"What are you talking about?"

"The girl you just now took to Ma's Kitchen," Babs said, still smiling. "Of course she's no beauty, so I guess I don't have anything to worry about. I am a beauty." She looked at him questioningly. "I'm not bragging, of course, but you do think so, don't you?"

He stood looking down at her upturned face, the red lips, the eager blue eyes, and he mentally admitted he had never met any other girl as bold and forthright as this Babs Ryan. She was a beauty, in a flamboyant sort of way. He couldn't deny that, but he wasn't as sure about her motives.

He sensed that Babs was dishonest, although he had no real evidence. It was just that he couldn't believe she was throwing herself at him because she liked him so much. He'd never been a great hand with the women, and the ones who had liked him were the quiet ones similar to Ann Dillon. Babs had some selfish motive of her own though he had no idea what it was.

"Sure, you're a beauty," he answered.

"Thank you." She pulled his head down and

kissed him on the lips. “I was a little afraid of what you’d say, hesitating the way you did.” She paused, and then asked, “Who is the girl?”

“Ann Dillon,” Johnny answered. “She’s the daughter of Al Dillon who fired at your pa last night.”

“So that’s it,” Babs said. “He’s a murderer, or tried to be. Like father, like daughter, I suppose.”

“No,” he said. “She’s not like him at all.”

“You sound as if you’re interested in her,” she said as she placed both hands on his arms and then slowly worked them upward toward his shoulders. “But you’re interested in me, aren’t you? I don’t have any real competition, do I?”

He found himself breathing hard again just as he had last night when she’d slipped into his tent. He had never met another woman who appealed to him physically the way Babs did, but he knew he could not afford to get mixed up with her. He had enough trouble without that. He’d have more trouble if he had an affair with her, pleasant as it might be.

“No, you don’t have any competition because I’m not interested in you,” he said and, jerking free from her hands, turned away.

“I’ll be in to see you again tonight,” she said. “I think you will be interested in me. I’m interested in you.”

He swung around, scowling at her. “Don’t come into my tent again tonight.”

She laughed. "Why, Mr. Lund, I believe you don't trust yourself, or me. Oh, there was one thing I wanted to ask. Have you found out anything more about the men who were associated with Dillon in his scheme to kill us? Who they were and how many or anything else?"

"No," he said, and walked away.

He did not look back, but he had a feeling she was laughing at him. She was a teaser, he thought angrily, and of all the kinds of women he disliked, he placed the teasers at the top. She might be doing it just for the hell of it, but on the other hand, she might have a reason for what she was doing. Maybe Chauncey Ryan had put her up to it.

He threaded his way through the wagons until he reached the Dillon camp. He looked around for anything on the ground that belonged to the Dillons, but he didn't find anything. He harnessed the Dillon horses and had started to hook them up when a man ran toward him, demanding, "Now just what the hell are you doing? Them horses belong to Al Dillon."

The man was stocky and deep-chested, maybe forty years old, with a yellow, downsweeping mustache. Johnny said, "Yes, I know. I'm not stealing the horses, if that's what's worrying you. I'm taking the wagon to Ma's Kitchen. Ann's working there and I thought she would want the wagon close so her things would be handy and she could sleep in it if she wants to."

"Oh, I didn't know she had a job," the man said. "I wondered where she'd gone."

He turned away. Johnny thought he had come from the wagon Ann said belonged to Chuck O'Leary. Maybe this fellow was O'Leary. Johnny called, "Wait."

The man turned to face him. "Well?"

"Are you Chuck O'Leary?"

"Yah, that's me," the man said, his eyes narrowing. "Why? You figure I done something? It was Dillon who fired that shot last night, not me."

"I know," Johnny said impatiently. "That's why Dillon's in jail, not you. I just want to talk to you. I'm going to take this wagon to Ma's Kitchen and leave it." He glanced at the sun. "It's close to noon, so I'll get my dinner while I'm there, then I'm coming back to talk to you. Stay here. I don't want to have to hunt for you."

The man's muddy brown eyes showed his fear, but he didn't panic and he didn't back up. He said, "All right, I'll be here if you just want to talk, only that's all you'd better do. I've got some friends in camp. If you try to throw me into the stinking jail to keep Dillon company, you'll find yourself in a hell of a lot of hot water."

"If you do something that makes it necessary to arrest you, I'll do it," Johnny said, "so don't try to bluff me with all of your friends."

"It ain't a bluff, Deputy," O'Leary said darkly. "Maybe you don't know it, but this camp is ready to explode right in your ugly mug. All it'll take is for you to make the wrong move."

"Stay here," Johnny said testily. "I'll be back before long. Like I said, I just want to talk to you."

He stepped up into the seat and drove to the road. He thought O'Leary was standing there staring after him, but he didn't look back to see. He had a strong feeling that O'Leary wasn't fooling about his friends. Johnny knew the man was right about one thing. The camp was ready to explode. All it would take was that one wrong move, and he might have to make it before evening.

CHAPTER X

Chauncey Ryan yawned and rubbed his eyes. Damn it, he wished he'd sat up last night and finished his paper work. He might as well have. He hadn't slept because he couldn't get his mind off that crazy killer, Al Dillon, who had taken a shot at him, and the young deputy, Johnny Lund, who maybe had saved his life by moving fast and preventing Dillon from shooting a second time.

On the other hand, Lund should have kept Dillon from taking the first shot. Most of all, Ryan's thoughts fastened on Plug Tully and his five gunslicks who were paid big money by the company to protect Ryan and Babs and so far hadn't been worth a nickel.

All night Ryan had had a terrifying feeling that in spite of anything he and Babs and Tebo Rand could do, this entire project was going to end up in blood and gunsmoke. He guessed it was George Mandell who bothered him the most. It took a strong man to pull this kind of thing off successfully, and Mandell was anything but a strong man.

Mandell was rich, but he was the most obnoxious old goat Ryan had ever run into, and Ryan had seen a lot of them. Apparently Mandell had never been in a rough camp like this before where saloons, brothels, and gambling halls were run wide open as they were here. He was fascinated. He had lost more money gambling than even a rich man could afford, he had been drinking too much, and he had spent far too much time in the brothels.

Ryan lit a cigar and walked to a window. He stood there watching Babs talk to the deputy, Johnny Lund, and couldn't help grinning. Babs had a way with men. A youngster like Lund was putty in her hands. She'd get in bed with him tonight and she'd set him on fire. If he knew anything about a conspiracy to kill Ryan and Babs and Mandell, she'd get it out of him.

The trouble was that Lund probably didn't know anything. The chances were Dillon was only a tool. If other men were involved in the murder attempt last night, Dillon might not know much about the scheme. Ryan hadn't met the man, but he had seen him, and he struck Ryan as the kind of innocent who would be used by smarter, craftier men.

Ryan was still standing by the window puffing on his cigar when Babs came back in. She didn't say anything, so he asked, "Well, what did you find out?"

"I found out that Deputy Johnny Lund doesn't want me to visit him tonight in his tent." She giggled. "He's just a kid, Chauncey, tempted by sin who is me but determined to prove he is stronger than the temptation."

"What about Dillon? Was he alone or did other men put him up to trying to kill me?"

She shrugged. "I didn't find out any more than I did last night. He doesn't know who they are, or at least he says he doesn't."

"Keep working on him," Ryan said. "Looked to me like you had him eating out of your hand."

"Not exactly," she said. "He reminds me of a chipmunk. He may be eating out of my hand, but he won't stand still for me to put my hand on him."

Ryan wasn't listening. He was watching Plug Tully walk along the street from one of the tent hotels. Ryan had never met a tougher man than Plug Tully, but toughness by itself was not enough. Tully just wasn't overbright. He was the kind who thought all problems could be solved by fists or a gun, so he would use one or the other when more than likely it was better to use his brain than either.

Tully turned when he reached the front of the house and walked into the room. He nodded at Babs. "Howdy, miss." Then he pinned his pale blue eyes on Ryan. He said, "I want to talk to Mandell."

"He's not up yet," Ryan said.

"The hell." Tully grinned knowingly. "He's still trying to outdo the young bucks, is he?"

"I dunno," Ryan answered. "You hear more about his capers than I do."

"I reckon I do," Tully agreed. "The girls say he's showing his age, but he gets a top grade for trying." He scowled, his knobby face showing his irritation. "Get him up. I don't figure on waiting. He ain't got no right to lay in bed till noon anyway."

Ryan nodded at Babs. "Get him up."

She nodded and climbed the stairs to Mandell's room. Neither Ryan nor Tully said a word while she was gone, but Ryan felt a strong personal dislike for the man. To have his life in the hands of a stupid gunslick like Plug Tully was unbearable. If he'd had his men scattered through the crowd the way he should have, Dillon would never have fired his shot.

Babs was laughing when she came back downstairs. She said, "He didn't want to get up. He said he'd just got to bed and he didn't believe me when I said it was noon."

"Well, is he up or ain't he?" Tully demanded. "If he ain't, I'm going up there and pull him out of bed and then say what I've got to say."

"Give him five minutes," Babs said. "He'll be down."

"Tonight you put your men in the crowd," Ryan said. "I refuse to get up on that platform if I'm not adequately protected."

"I don't give a damn whether you're on the

platform or not," Tully said in a surly tone.

Again there was silence until Mandell came slowly down the stairs. He needed a shave and his eyes were bloodshot and he had trouble staying on his feet. Ryan suspected he had a whacking headache and was probably dizzy to boot. The dignity that he always wore like an expensive coat when he was completely sober was gone. He looked like a sick old man, Ryan thought with distaste, and that was exactly what he was.

"What is it, Tully?" Mandell asked as he dropped into a chair and put a hand to his forehead. "I didn't intend to get up this early. What you have to say had better be important."

"Oh, it is, Mandell," Tully said. "Believe me, it is. While I'm talking, old man, I'll give you some advice. You've lived without sin all these years, I guess, judging from the way you're lapping it up now. Don't try to make up for it in one week. You'll kill yourself trying."

Mandell's face darkened with anger. He wanted to be called *Mister* Mandell by an underling like Plug Tully, and he didn't want to be called an old man. He didn't seek advice from the gunman, either, particularly the kind of advice Tully had just given him.

He fought his temper for a moment, but he felt too sick to make an issue out of it, so he said mildly enough, "Thanks for your advice, Tully. Now what did you want to see me about?"

Tully shot a glance at Ryan to see how he was reacting. He probably thought, Ryan told himself, that he could browbeat Mandell, but he recognized the fact that Chauncey Ryan had knocked around the West too much to be battered into submission by Tully or any other tough hand. George Mandell was something else, and Tully had recognized his weakness the same as Ryan had.

Tully waited, letting the silence spin out which in turn tightened the tension, then he said slowly and deliberately, "I'm pulling my men off the job. We're riding out right after we get dinner in Ma's Kitchen. We want our time."

For a moment there was silence again, the tension tighter than ever. Even Ryan who had expected almost anything from the man, was shocked. Babs simply stared at him open-mouthed, as if she just couldn't believe what she had heard. Mandell seemed to be the least concerned of the three.

"You can't do that," Babs cried. "We were promised adequate protection or we would never have taken the job."

"That's right," Ryan said angrily, "and by God, you sure didn't give it to us. I'm all for getting you off the job, but you've got to stay until we find replacements. You're better than nothing. Not much, but a little."

Tully ignored the insult. He was watching

Mandell, completely ignoring Babs and Ryan. "They're dead wrong," he said. "We're leaving and we want our time."

Mandell reached into his coat pocket and drew out a meerschaum pipe and a can of Prince Albert and began dribbling tobacco into the bowl. "I don't think you're doing anything of the kind, Tully. Two reasons. Number One. I wouldn't give you a cent if you pull your boys off the job now with most of the drawing still to come."

He tamped the tobacco down and slipped the can back into his pocket, then fished around for a match. Ryan was astonished as he watched Mandell who appeared to be in no hurry at all. Mandell added, "By the way, why did you decide you wanted to pull out of a good-paying job like this one?"

"Too risky," Tully said hoarsely. "This ain't the first time I've been around crowds before they became mobs. I know the signs. It's a smell in the air, a kind of feeling you get. By tonight or tomorrow at the latest something will change these men into a murdering mob. All three of you will be killed if you're still here. So will my men and I if we stay, which we ain't."

"That's one of the things you're supposed to keep from happening," Mandell said. "Stop it."

"Stop it?" Tully stared at him as if he were crazy. "How do you expect six men to stop five hundred?"

"I'm sure I don't know," Mandell said easily, "but you're supposed to be the expert, so you should know."

"I don't," Tully snapped, "and I ain't staying around to find out."

"I suspect you're not the tough hand we thought we had hired," Mandell said. "You'd never make a Texas Ranger. Maybe you've heard the story about the Ranger who was sent to put down a riot. When he reached the town where the riot was, they asked him where the rest of the Rangers were. He said, 'There's just one riot, ain't there?' All right, we'll have only one mob."

"We ain't Texas Rangers and that's a fact," Tully said. "By the time we get done working you over, I think you'll be glad to let us have the money we've got coming. Don't make us do that."

Mandell grinned around his pipestem, then busied himself striking a match and firing the tobacco. He puffed a few times before he said, "I have no intention of making you do it, Tully. You haven't heard my Number Two reason. Remember that I'm on the board of half a dozen railroads and some mining companies, and I have many friends on the boards of other companies, companies that hire men like you for various kinds of guard duty. I can pull more strings than you ever thought of."

He paused and puffed some more. Tully said

roughly, "Well, you ain't proved anything to me yet."

"Why, I thought you saw my point," Mandell said. "All right, I'll make it plain enough so even you will savvy. If you walk out on this job, I'll see to it that you never get a job anywhere else. I'll blackball you, Tully. You'll be finished. You'll be out of work as long as you live unless you want to try a pick and shovel."

"The hell," Tully breathed.

For the first time since Ryan had met Mandell, he had some respect for the man. Too, for the first time he had some understanding of what had brought him to the top in the industrial jungle. He was a tough fighter in a clinch, tougher than Ryan had guessed.

"Now you'd better get out of here and go tell your boys you're staying right here in Mallard City until I can get replacements for you," Mandell said. "I'll wire headquarters immediately, but it may take a few days to find the right men."

"All right, we'll stay a few more days," Tully said in a surly tone and, wheeling, strode out of the room.

Mandell pulled on his pipe, watching Tully until he disappeared down the street, then he rose. "Babs, my head is killing me this morning. Have you got any coffee on the stove?"

She nodded. "There's about half a pot."

"Good." He walked into the kitchen, then stopped and looked back. "Oh, I forgot to tell you, Ryan. I'll be on the platform with you tonight like you asked." He went on into the kitchen then and Ryan heard him getting a cup out of the cupboard.

"Well," Babs said softly, "what do you think of that?"

"I think I was wrong about him," Ryan said. "It's something I learned a long time ago, but I keep forgetting it."

"What's that?" she asked.

"You never can tell how far a frog can jump by measuring the length of his legs," Ryan answered.

CHAPTER XI

Johnny drove the Dillon wagon around Ma's Kitchen to the back of the tent. Billy Bean was using a bucksaw on a fair-sized pine log. The chunk dropped off as Johnny stepped down. Billy straightened and wiped a sleeve across his sweaty face.

"Where'd you find that broken-down old team of nags?" Billy asked. "And that wagon? Looks to me like it's held together by spit and baling wire."

Johnny grinned. "More spit than wire. It belongs to Ann's father, so now you've an idea of the kind of man he is."

"I reckon so." Billy shook his head. "I don't see how he ever got this far with it."

"Neither do I," Johnny said. "How's Ann making out?"

"She's making out real good," Billy said. "I think she satisfies Ma and that's quite a trick. She's a working fiend, that woman. I'd have been better off signing on with Ed Neal and pinning a star on my shirt. Then I wouldn't have to work my tail off the way I'm doing now."

"That's right," Johnny agreed affably. "You wouldn't have to do a damned thing, but then you'd only make half as much as you're making now. You'd be risking your neck bucking the company and Plug Tully and his men on one side and five hundred mean-tempered settlers on the other." He paused, and then asked, "You want to trade?"

"Well, no," Billy said, "now that you put it that way. Maybe I'm just as well off as you are. Say, I'll unharness and stake them horses out for you if you'll grab hold of this bucksaw. You need some exercise."

"Yeah, I guess I do," Johnny said. "I'm getting soft. It'll perk up my appetite."

Johnny sawed two chunks off the log while Billy took care of the horses. He was glad to get free of the bucksaw when Billy returned. "That's hard work," he said. "I don't see how you keep ahead of the big range Ma's got in there."

"It's all I can do," Billy said. "Ann being here helps. Before that I was running around like I was loco, with Ma yelling at me to run faster."

Johnny laughed. "You got yourself into this fix," he said. "I've got no call to feel sorry for you."

He went into the tent through the back. Ann was sitting at the counter eating her dinner. Ma, standing at the range, was frying steak. Johnny called, "I'll have that steak, Ma."

She glowered at him. "Oh, no you won't. You'll wait your turn like everybody else."

The rush was over. Only three men sat at the

counter waiting for their dinner. Johnny took the seat beside Ann, asking, "How'd my girl make out this morning, Ma?"

"Your girl?" Ann cried as if she was shocked. "When did I get to be your girl?"

"I won you by combat," he said. "Remember?"

"Yes, but . . ."

"I got you your job, didn't I?"

"Yes, but . . ."

"All right," Johnny said triumphantly. "That makes me your fellow and makes you my girl. What's more, I'm ready and able to bash in the head of the first man who tries to beat my time."

"Are you now?" Ann said. "Don't I get asked about it?"

"Of course not," Johnny said.

Ma glanced over her shoulder at them. "She done fine this morning, Johnny. Now if you two love birds are done fluttering around and if you're finished, Ann, I'll sit down and have my dinner. I've been standing over this stove and smelling this food and not eating, and now my tapeworm is hollering."

Ann rose. "I'm done, Ma. I think it's dangerous to sit here beside this madman anyhow."

"Naw," Ma said. "He's all bluff."

"I'll ignore that remark," Johnny said. "Ann, I brought your wagon to the back of the tent. I figured there were some things in it you'd want and maybe you'd like to sleep in it tonight."

"Thank you," Ann said.

After he finished eating, Johnny dropped a coin on the counter. When Ann came to him to pick up the money, he said, "I met your neighbor, Chuck O'Leary. He objected to me harnessing up your pa's team. I guess he thought I was trying to steal the horses."

She smiled. "As if those worn-out old horses were worth stealing."

"I convinced him I was honest," Johnny said, "and I told him to stay where he was. I'd come back and talk to him. He objected to that, too."

"Just how are you planning to talk to him?" Ann asked.

"With my six-shooter if I have to use it to get some answers," Johnny said.

Instinctively she reached across the counter and gripped his arm. "Johnny, these are honest men. I don't know them by name, but I've seen some of them gather around O'Leary's wagon and talk. Pa spent a lot of time with them. They're wrong to think they can make everything right with a lynching, but all they want is a square deal."

"I've got to keep the peace," Johnny said.

"I know that, but please be careful," she said. "They don't trust you because they think you're on the company's side. I mean, it would be a terrible thing if you were killed by decent men who get carried away with their anger, and the real crooks aren't hurt at all."

"I aim to look out for Number One," Johnny said, and glanced down at her hand.

She drew it back, blushing. She said in a low tone, "I never had many friends in my whole life. I don't want to lose any that I have."

"I feel the same way," he agreed, winking at her. "I don't want to be lost."

He left the tent, noticing that Plug Tully and his men had just walked in and were sitting at the counter. He ignored them and they gave him the same treatment. He wondered about Tully as he moved along the street and then turned into the camp and threaded his way through the wagons to O'Leary's.

Tully had backed down last night when Johnny had refused to turn Dillon over to him. Would he do it again? And would he use his men to better advantage than he had last night? Johnny didn't know, but he distrusted Tully even more than he did Chauncey Ryan.

When he approached O'Leary's wagon, he saw that two other men were hunkered beside his campfire, smoking and talking, but when they saw Johnny coming toward them, they rose and walked away. O'Leary continued to puff his pipe, scowling at Johnny who squatted beside him.

"You kept me waiting long enough," he grumbled.

"I had to wait a while for my dinner at Ma's

Kitchen," Johnny said. "What's the matter with your friends? I'm not poison."

"You are to them," O'Leary said ominously. "I'm guessing you're gonna be poison to me. Maybe you ain't getting paid by the company the way Tully and his bunch of toughs are, but it adds up to the same thing."

"How do you figure that?"

"You ain't seeing to it that we get an honest draw," O'Leary said resentfully. "That's why Al Dillon took a shot at Ryan last night. He thought a different man might be honest. It sure is a shame he's a rotten shot."

This was typical short-range thinking, Johnny told himself. It never occurred to these people that there was no way he could guarantee an honest draw, or that up to now no one had proved the draw wasn't honest. Or that it was to their interest as well as the company's that law and order be kept in the camp.

He saw no purpose in arguing with O'Leary. The man would never be convinced against his will. Johnny said, "Al Dillon named you as the man who gave him the revolver he used last night."

"He's lying," O'Leary said, tight-lipped.

"I don't think so," Johnny said. "Ann told me her father did not have a gun, so you or somebody had to give it to him. You're as good a bet as any, being a neighbor to him like you were."

"Wasn't me," O'Leary said, staring at the fire.

"Then who was it?"

"How would I know?"

Johnny felt anger warming him. He was in no mood to be stalled, and the stupid, childish attitude O'Leary was showing was more than Johnny would put up with. He guessed the vast majority of the settlers felt the same way, and if he didn't get the truth now, he probably never would. He had to know what was being planned if he was going to stop it. He guessed that another attempt on Ryan's or Mandell's life would be made, and he wasn't sure he could stop it even if he did know.

"Dillon said it was you and I don't believe Dillon was lying," Johnny said. "He had no reason to. Now, are you going to tell me who else is involved in this scheme?"

"Who's going to make me?" O'Leary growled. "You ain't man enough to do it."

Johnny pulled his gun. He said, "O'Leary, you have a fine set of teeth for a fellow your age. Did you ever see what a man looks like when his teeth are knocked out by the barrel of a .45? Snaggle-tooth is what they're going to call you in about five seconds if you don't tell me what I want to know."

"Aw, you wouldn't do any . . ."

Johnny was balancing on his toes. Now he launched himself at O'Leary, his gun barrel cracking the settler on his head. It was not a hard enough blow to knock him out, but it hurt. He spilled backwards, Johnny on top of him, the gun barrel raised for a second blow.

"Your teeth," Johnny said. "Every tooth you've got showing in the front of your head."

O'Leary believed him this time. He muttered, "Hold it." He swallowed and added, "I don't know all the men who are in it any more'n Dillon did. All I know is that Norman Bradford is ramrodding the show. He knows who Ryan and the woman are."

Johnny got up and holstered his gun. "On your feet, bucko," he said. "You're taking me to your friend Bradford. Pronto."

CHAPTER XII

O'Leary held a sullen silence as he led Johnny through the wagons to Norman Bradford's camp. The sullenness and the anger were not just in O'Leary. Johnny felt it all around him. He saw it in the eyes of the men and women who watched him as he walked by their wagons. Two men spit in his direction. Another man tossed a cigar stub in front of him with a violent, angry motion.

None of the men threatened him or even said anything. One woman did, a tall, gray-haired virago who screamed at her husband, "Ain't that the bastard who arrested Al Dillon last night? You oughtta cut him into little pieces."

By now Dillon was probably the best-known man in camp, and this woman would have said, like O'Leary, that she was sorry Dillon wasn't a better shot. She would likely have added that murder was justified under these circumstances and that Johnny was taking the company's side when he arrested Dillon.

Johnny was reminded of the sultry feeling that pervades the air just before a violent thunder-storm. Only a poor caliber of gullible people would have swallowed the company's bait and come here seeking a fortune for the relatively small price of a ticket, poor and shiftless people who were constantly seeking something for nothing.

Dillon was typical of them, although his team and wagon were the worst Johnny had seen. The only wonder was that Ann could have been a part of such a crowd, but if it hadn't been for her father, she would never have been here.

"This is it," O'Leary said in a sullen tone. "You try getting tough with Norman Bradford and every man in camp will come on the run. You'll get tossed out on your butt and you'll get your noggin cracked to boot."

A man and woman were sitting by their fire. A tow-headed girl about four or five was playing with a woolly-haired pup back of the wagon. The man rose when he saw O'Leary and Johnny turn toward him, a tall man with a square jaw and a black mustache and a good pair of shoulders.

Johnny instantly had a feeling that this fellow had landed up in the wrong place. He bore no resemblance to Dillon or O'Leary or any of the other men in the raggle-taggle crowd that had assembled here.

"Norm," O'Leary said, "this here young squirt is Lund, the deputy you've seen strutting around camp. He claimed he wanted to talk to you. Lund, meet Norm Bradford."

Johnny extended his hand and Bradford gripped it, his blue eyes searching Johnny's face. His grip was firm, his gaze did not slide off to one side, and suddenly Johnny realized that Norman Bradford was very much a man.

"One thing I can always do is talk, Mr. Lund," Bradford said. "Come on over to the fire. Not that we need a fire on a warm day like this, but it's pleasant to have one."

"I didn't want to bring him," O'Leary said somberly, "but he was gonna knock out all my teeth if I didn't. I believe the bastard would have done it."

It was apparent that Bradford had trouble restraining a grin. He was silent a moment as he fought his sense of humor, then he said, "Well now, Chuck, you're a bigger man than he is, looks like. I don't think I'd let him do that if I was you."

"If I was you, I wouldn't, either," O'Leary said angrily, "but I ain't you, and mebbe I ain't as tough as this young rooster. Anyhow, he's here, and I'll be obliged if you'll knock a few of his teeth out."

"Oh, I won't have any trouble with him," Bradford said, "and he won't have any trouble with me. I'm glad you brought him, Chuck, and that you've still got your teeth."

O'Leary grunted an obscenity, then wheeled and strode away. Bradford laughed softly, and said, "Well, come on to the fire, Mr. Lund. This is my wife Martha. And our only child, Delight. We were both over forty when she arrived, so Delight seemed the natural name for her."

Mrs. Bradford shook hands with Johnny, asking, "Will you have a cup of coffee, Mr. Lund? We keep the pot on the fire all day. It seems that we're spoiled, just sitting here with nothing to do, so we drink lots of coffee."

"Yes, I'd like to have a cup," Johnny said.

Delight had turned from her puppy. She said clearly, "How do you do, Mr. Lund?"

"I'm pleased to meet you, Delight," Johnny said. "What's your dog's name?"

"We call him Job," the little girl said. "His mother and brothers and sisters all died on the way out here, so Papa said he should be called Job because he suffered so much sorrow. You know there was a man in the Bible named Job who suffered a lot of sorrow."

She turned back to the puppy. Johnny asked, "How old is she, Mr. Bradford?"

"Four."

"She acts older," Johnny said. "I've got a niece and a nephew who are both older, but they act younger than she does."

"I'm sure Delight acts older than most children her age," Bradford said. "Since she's our only child and since we were married almost twenty years before she came along, I guess we don't really treat her as if she's a child."

Mrs. Bradford came with a tin cup of steaming coffee and handed it to Johnny. He said, "Thank you." He turned to Bradford again. "I'll tell you why I'm here. As you know, Al Dillon tried to murder Chauncey Ryan last night. I have him in jail now. His daughter tells me he did not have a gun. I finally persuaded him to tell me how he got the gun. He said O'Leary gave it to him and that other men were involved in the plan to kill Ryan. That's where the teeth business came in. It was my way of persuading O'Leary to tell me who knew about the plot and he named you."

"There is one major error there as far as I'm concerned," Bradford said. "I do not know of any plan or plot to murder anybody. I didn't know that O'Leary had given Dillon a gun, and I don't approve of him taking advantage of a man like Dillon and working him into the kind of hopeless rage that leads to murder. As I said, it was done without my approval."

Johnny sipped his coffee and studied Bradford over the rim of the cup. For the first time he felt his youth and inexperience, and he was suddenly resentful. Here was a man who in no way resembled the shiftless men who had gathered here in Mallard City hoping for something for practically nothing. He seemed to be a steady, thoughtful man, a solid citizen completely without guile.

It just didn't add up any way Johnny looked at it. He began to wonder if he was failing to size Bradford up right, if the man was really as straightforward and honest as he judged him to be. It was just possible, Johnny told himself, that Norman Bradford was making a fool out of him.

"Well then, maybe you can tell me what's going on," Johnny said finally. "Trouble is building up and I want it stopped before it gets too big to be stopped. There's a lot of talk about a crooked draw. I don't know how the talk started or who started it, but I do know we're going to have a lynching or maybe more than one if we don't stop it pronto."

"I am not in favor of a lynching," Bradford said quickly, "but if there is one, I suppose I'm responsible. You see, I'm the one who started the talk about the crooked draw because I'm convinced we're having one."

Johnny drew a long breath. So now he knew the answer to one question, and he felt as he had at first, that Bradford was an honest man. He said, "Would you explain that?"

"Certainly," Bradford said. "I believe I am the only man in camp who knows about Ryan and his woman Babs. Of course others know now because I've told a number of them . . ."

"Now wait a minute," Johnny interrupted. "You said Ryan's woman. Babs is his daughter. I know she's not as young as she pretends to be, but that doesn't make her his woman."

Bradford nodded. "I'll explain how I know about them. I'm a fairly wealthy man, at least compared to most of the men in camp. Not long ago I sold my farm in Ohio and took a river steamboat to New Orleans to look into a business proposition I had heard of down there. Ryan and Babs were on the boat. They were gamblers, working together, but Babs was the slick one. I tell you she's a magician with cards."

He paused and grinned as if he were ashamed of himself. "I'll be the first to admit that they took me in. I lost several hundred dollars before I figured out what was happening. I couldn't prove it, but I'm convinced that she dealt Ryan the winning hands and I think she knew every card she gave each one of us."

Johnny stared at Bradford, shocked and only half believing what the man had told him. "You couldn't be mistaken about their identity?"

"Oh no," Bradford said. "Not at all. There's more, too. Later a man got on the boat at Memphis who swore that they had run a badger game on him. He tried to get his money back from Ryan. It worked into a gunfight and Ryan shot and killed the man. Of course Ryan denied any knowledge of a badger game, but after sitting at a poker table with them, I believe the story."

"Why are they passing Babs off as his daughter?" Johnny asked.

Bradford shrugged. "Who knows? I suppose they figured it was the kind of arrangement that would look good and make people trust them, a father and daughter situation. She's attractive and adds beauty and color to the drawing. One thing about Ryan. He's a good showman. That's probably why he was hired."

Bradford pointed a forefinger at Johnny and waggled it at him. "I can't prove to you that the drawing is crooked, but I ask you what kind of a company would hire a pair like that? If they're crooked, then the company is composed of men who are crooks or fools."

Johnny nodded, still not wanting to believe what Bradford had said. He asked, "You want a delay to have new people sent here by the company to run the drawing?"

"That's exactly right," Bradford agreed. "I don't trust the company after seeing George Mandell and Plug Tully in addition to Ryan and the woman, but my feeling is that if we showed we are not as gullible as the company considered us, they would send better people the next time."

"They might," Johnny said, "but if this crowd turns into a mob, there'll be killings. It's hard to tell where it will stop. The whole thing will backfire, Mr. Bradford."

"I know, and I promise I will do all I can to stop it," Bradford said. "I didn't bargain for a mob when I started telling people about Ryan and the woman, but the signs are all around us now. I may have created a monster that I did not intend to create."

"You'll be at the drawing tonight?"

"Of course."

Johnny handed the empty cup to Mrs. Bradford. "Thanks for the coffee," he said. "Good-by, Delight."

"Good-by, Mr. Lund," the girl said.

"You're more than welcome to the coffee," Mrs. Bradford said, then lowered her voice so the girl couldn't hear. "Believe me, Mr. Lund, we're frightened. We don't want a riot any more than you do."

"That's right," Bradford said. "I just didn't realize until it was too late what I was doing. I think we can control the situation, but there are some firebrands in the crowd, and we can't be sure how much harm they can do, as angry as the men are."

"Is it your notion that the company is trying to cheat you by controlling the drawing in some way?" Johnny asked. "Like giving the Cross Heart to one of their own people and making it impossible for any of you folks to get a chance to draw it?"

"Either that," Bradford said, "or they have made a deal with one of the settlers to get it and have been paid extra by that particular settler. Of course we can't overlook the possibility that Ryan has made a deal for himself. It's quite possible the company is not involved. My feeling comes from knowing about Ryan and the woman.

I just don't think that people who are basically dishonest are going to handle this kind of thing honestly."

"How did you get involved in a scheme like this?" Johnny asked. "It's a sucker game and you're smart enough to recognize it."

"No, I'm afraid I wasn't," Bradford admitted ruefully. "At least I wasn't when I bought the tickets, five of them. The $500 didn't hurt me, although I would like to have it back. You see, after I returned from New Orleans—the deal down there didn't work out for me—we decided to come out to Oregon and look around for something. I hadn't heard of this drawing until I go to Alturas. I ran into a good salesman and I believed all of his lies about it not being possible to lose and there was the chance I could hit it lucky by drawing the Cross Heart. That was the bait he kept dangling in front of me."

"It only proves one thing," Mrs. Bradford said sourly. "My smart husband is not as smart as he thought he was."

"I'll have to admit it," Bradford said. "She informed me I was a fool as soon as I told her about buying the tickets. She was dead right, but after being a fool, I want a chance at the Cross Heart. Or some of the timber if I can't get the ranch."

"I'll watch the drawing tonight," Johnny said.

He nodded at them and walked away. By the

time he reached the road, a question rose in his mind. Was there some way Bradford could profit by creating a riot, or delaying the draw for a few days? He found no answer, but the question continued to nag him.

He guessed that the question stemmed from the obvious fact that Norman Bradford was very smooth. This had not occurred to him when he was with Bradford, but now that he was away from the man's magnetic presence, he realized that Norman Bradford was the kind who could charm you right out of your eye teeth and that had just about happened to him.

CHAPTER XIII

Sheriff Ed Neal woke from a sound sleep to hear someone hammering on his front door. He turned over, thinking that if he didn't get up, whoever was out there would go away, but he was wrong. The hammering continued.

Neal threw the covers back and put his feet on the cold floor. He cursed and pulled his pants on, then his slippers. He shook his head and got up. It was still black dark. He fumbled around on the bureau until he found a box of matches. He struck one and lit the lamp near his bed.

Whoever was out there pounding on the front door had a hell of a hard fist, he thought sourly. He bellowed, "I'm coming, damn it, I'm coming."

He picked up the lamp and left the bedroom. He had planned to go fishing today with Chick Robbins, the owner of the Piute hardware store. It would be a three-day trip to Steens Mountain, one day down, one day fishing, and one day back.

His first thought was that Chick had not understood the time they were to start and had expected Neal to be up before dawn. He discarded the idea immediately. Chick was a great sleeper, and he wasn't one to get out of his warm bed at this hour if he could help it.

Neal was not a man to have premonitions, but

as he crossed the front room, he had the feeling that his fishing trip was going up in smoke.

He had put the trip off all summer, largely because his wife didn't want him to go, but she had taken the northbound stage to Canyon City a couple of days ago to visit her sister. He couldn't pass up a chance like that, so he had immediately gone to the hardware store and started making plans for the fishing trip with Chick Robbins.

He gripped the knob of the front door, hesitating. There had been many times since he had been elected sheriff when he had been tempted to say to hell with it and saddle up his horse and ride out of the country. At this moment, and there had been many moments like it, he wondered why he had ever thought he wanted to be sheriff.

Suppose he blew out the lamp and went back to bed? Sooner or later whoever was barking his knuckles would get tired and go away, and then he could go fishing with Chick. He sighed and told himself that no man was ever completely free. He had no choice. He might just as well accept his responsibility and remember how he felt so he wouldn't be tempted to run for sheriff again when his term was out.

He turned the knob and pulled the door open. Old Sam Gates, the telegrapher, stood there with a telegram in his hand. He asked, "My God, Sheriff, does it take an earthquake to wake you up?"

"No," Neal answered in a grumpy tone. "Just a man knocking on my front door."

"I thought I was doing you a favor." Gates handed the telegram to Neal. "Looked to me like you'd want this."

Gates wheeled and strode away in the darkness. Neal shut the door and set the lamp on the claw-footed, oak stand in the center of the room. He read: "Mallard City. Sheriff Ed Neal, Piute, Oregon. Your presence in Mallard City is essential at once. Attempt was made on the life of Chauncey Ryan last night. Bloody riot is threatened. Your young deputy Lund cannot hold the lid on much longer. George Mandell, Representative of the Cascade and Snake River Wagon Road Grant Company."

Neal sat down in the nearest chair and cursed for three minutes straight hand running. He had told Johnny Lund that it was his job and he was not to ask for help. He was to handle it himself. Neal had made it absolutely clear without qualification. He would not leave Piute.

He ran his hand over his face and took a deep breath. Well, Johnny hadn't asked for help, but the wagon road grant people had. Apparently this fellow Mandell had no confidence in Johnny or he would not have sent the telegram.

Again the thought came to Neal that he could forget the whole business and go on a fishing trip, and again he knew he could not. Suppose a riot did break out and there was bloodshed? Johnny was a good man, but he was young and inexperienced. Men would die because of that inexperience, and when it was all over, he, Ed Neal, would be to blame for what had happened.

He could resent it until there was a frosty night in hell; but that wouldn't change the basic fact that he should have gone to Mallard City in the first place. He was sheriff, it was his responsibility, and the blame for the lives and property that were lost would rest on his shoulders in spite of all the squirming around he did. *He would be to blame.* The words kept running through his mind. He knew he had no choice—he had to go to Mallard City.

He took the lamp back to the bedroom and finished dressing, buckled his gun belt around his waist, and picked up his Winchester from where he had leaned it against the wall. It was a long ride to Mallard City and he was not looking forward to it. He would do well to get there by sundown.

When Neal left the house through the back door, the first opalescent light of dawn had worked up into the eastern sky. He saddled his black gelding, shoved the rifle into the boot, and mounted.

It took five minutes to ride to Chick Robbins' house and another five minutes to get him out of bed and tell him the fishing trip was off. Robbins bellowed, "You can't do this. We've made plans. This is the first time your wife left town in three years. She won't let you go after she gets back. Tell the damn land company to go to hell."

Neal turned and strode back to his horse. He knew how Robbins felt and he wished he could do exactly what Robbins said.

He stepped into the saddle and rode south, mentally admitting he was just dreaming. The sun came up into a clear sky and his long shadow ran beside him. Most of the country was a high desert, covered by sage with some grass and a few gnarled and ancient juniper trees. It was rolling, but occasionally he came to canyons he had to cross. It took time to find breaks in the rimrock and work his way to the bottom, and more time to find a way out.

He made no effort to keep on the road which twisted and turned and added fifty miles to the journey. Now he wondered if he would have been ahead in the long run to have stayed on the road.

Near noon he reached the Bar C. He had dinner there, then asked for and was given a fresh horse, a good-looking, leggy bay, but within the hour he realized he should have kept his black, tired as the horse was. In the middle of the afternoon he came to the Rafter A.

He stopped for a drink of water and wangled another horse, a buckskin that had the staying qualities the bay had lacked. This animal would get him to Mallard City in time and he felt better. He'd have to ride hard if he was going to reach his destination before dark.

The sun was almost down when he reached the tent town. He had not been here for several months and he was unprepared for what he saw. He was amazed at the number of people who were camped here, the wagons and horses and tents that seemed to run on and on.

When he came to the old ranch house, he saw the sign that said it was the company office. He realized that this was a far bigger operation than he had guessed, and he felt guilty. He had been foolish to send Johnny Lund down here alone to keep an eye on things.

He had no idea what the trouble was that had impelled Mandell to wire him, but where there were this many people, all transient, and many of them predators who lived off other men, there was bound to be plenty of work for lawmen.

He reined up in front of the ranch house, tied at the hitch rail, and strode up the path and into the house. A big, handsome man wearing a calfskin vest sat at a desk thumbing through a stack of papers, a pretty blond young woman, actually a girl, Neal thought, came out of the kitchen in the rear of the house and stood smiling at him in a provocative way that both stirred and irritated him.

"I'm Sheriff Ed Neal from Piute," Neal said.

"I'm here because I received a wire from a man named George Mandell who claimed I was needed here."

The big man rose. "We're glad you came, Sheriff. I'm Chauncey Ryan." He motioned to the girl. "My daughter Babs."

Neal shook hands with Ryan, then with the girl who had moved toward him in a graceful, hip-swinging manner that made him wonder if she was the cause of the trouble. Neal said, "I want to see Mandell. I've got some questions to ask him concerning the wire he sent me."

Ryan nodded at the girl. "He's in his room, Babs. Have him come down."

The girl nodded and ran up the stairs. Ryan dropped into his chair and leaned back, pinning his gaze on Neal's chunky body. He said, "You look like a competent lawman."

"I consider myself one," Neal said, irritated by the note of arrogance in Ryan's voice.

A moment later a tall, white-haired man came down the stairs. He said, "I'm George Mandell. I sent the wire."

Neal shook hands with him, catching the strong, whisky smell about him and instinctively disliking him. He said sharply, "I sent a deputy to see that law and order was maintained during the drawing. I did not intend to be here because there are other matters for a sheriff to do in a big county like this and he should stay in the county seat. Now I want to know what Lund has done that made it necessary for you to send the wire."

"Why, Lund hasn't done anything," Mandell said as if surprised. "We have no criticism of him. It's simply that we're sitting on a volcano that may erupt any time. We need an older head, that's all."

"And a second man, Sheriff," Ryan added smoothly. "The settlers will listen to a sheriff when they won't pay any attention to a kid deputy."

Neal backed up to the wall and sat down in a rawhide-bottom chair. He started to swear, then remembered the girl, and stopped. He said in a clipped tone, "You mean to tell me that Lund has not made any mistakes, that you simply wanted the sheriff instead of a deputy?"

"Let's say the sheriff and his deputy," Mandell said. "This is a big thing, Sheriff. Five hundred men are camped here. A huge land grant is being divided among them. A ranch that's worth a fortune. Hundreds of acres of valuable timber land. It won't take much to start a riot. I don't want that to happen. It's my opinion you are needed here for the next few days, not in Piute."

"I was shot at last night." Ryan motioned to the girl. "Babs and I were on the platform. It's up to you to protect us. We think there may be another attempt on our lives tonight. I don't propose to be a sitting duck for some disgruntled idiot who's sore because he didn't draw the Cross Heart, and I don't propose to expose Babs to that kind of danger, either."

Neal looked from one to the other, then he said angrily, "Well, by God, if you think I'm your errand boy to come running whenever you wiggle a finger at me, you're loco. I shouldn't even have sent Johnny Lund down here. It's your show, so furnish your own protection."

"It's not enough," Mandell said. "We are selling property we own. We have a right to be protected by the law."

"All right, I'm here," Neal said, "but I'm leaving in the morning. As long as Johnny Lund can handle things, he can stay if he wants. I'll talk to him."

He had no intention of going back in the morning, but it was just as well they thought he was. It made him furious that company men were arrogant enough to think that all they had to do was to send him a wire and he'd come on the run. It made him even more furious that he had done exactly that. The fact that this was typical of a big land company didn't help his feelings.

He rose and turned to the door. He'd get the real story from Johnny. It just might be he'd take Johnny back to Piute. It would serve these bastards right if he did.

"No, Sheriff," the girl said. "Don't leave in the morning. This is more serious than you think. If you go back and there is a riot, a lot of people will be killed and the tents and houses burned and the women, including me, raped. You were elected to prevent trouble, not to shift the responsibility to the shoulders of a young deputy." She paused, and then, her eyes still pinned directly on him, she added, "I can't see inside your head, but was there a reason for you sending Johnny Lund instead of coming yourself? Is it possible you were afraid?"

Ryan and Mandell were staring at him, too. Ryan said, "It makes a man wonder, doesn't it, Sheriff?"

Neal had wheeled back to face the girl. Now he looked at Ryan, then at Mandell. He sat down again. "All right," he said. "I figure you're going to lie to me, but I'll listen anyhow."

CHAPTER XIV

Johnny Lund glanced into Ma's Kitchen, having no intention of going in if the tent was as crowded as it had been earlier in the day, but it wasn't. Only six men were eating their supper, so Johnny went in and moved around the counter to the back where he could be by himself. He had hoped that Ann Dillon would come and sit beside him, but he was still pleasantly surprised when she did come the instant she saw him.

"I want to talk to you," she said.

"Good," he said. "That's just what I want."

Ma saw him then and called, "Steak again, Johnny?"

"Right," he said.

"Get him a cup of coffee, Ann," Ma said. "I'll put a steak on for you, too. You might as well have your supper now. I don't figure we'll have another rush like we did this morning. Most of our customers are gonna get along on two meals today, darn it."

Ann sighed. "I'll get your coffee."

Ma moved over to her work table to finish the apple pie she had started. "You fetched me a good girl, Johnny," she said. "She's worked like a horse all day. I didn't think young women wanted to work any more, not like we did when I was that age, but Ann's all right."

Ann brought two cups of coffee and sat down beside Johnny again. She was breathing hard as if she had just come in from a hard run. He looked at her, not certain if she was tired enough to breathe that way, or whether she was scared of something.

"I've got to talk to you," she said in a low voice, "if Ma will just let me alone for a minute. We've had a steady run of customers all day. Most of them are settlers, and so we've heard a lot of their talk . . ."

Billy Bean came in through the rear of the tent with an armload of wood. He threw it down with a great clatter. "Well, if it ain't the law. Who are you after this time, me or that good-looking girl who's sitting beside you?"

"Go on back to your saw, Billy," Ann said. "Can't you see I'm trying to talk to him?"

"Oh, I don't want to go back to my saw yet." Billy wiped his face with a sleeve. "I'm tired. I think I'll trade jobs with you, Johnny. Give me the star and I'll . . ."

"I'll give you something if you don't get out of here," Ann said.

Billy sighed. "I guess you've got the inside track with that filly, Johnny. I've been trying to get somewhere with her all day, but her mind just ain't on me."

"Give me your gun, Johnny," Ann said. "I can see I'm going to have to remove a pest."

"All right, all right," Billy said hastily. "I'm leaving," and disappeared through the back of the tent.

Ma returned to the range to inspect the meat. "Yes sir, Johnny," she said, "Ann's a good worker. Was I you, I wouldn't let her get away from me."

Johnny winked at Ann who now was thoroughly angry. He said out of the corner of his mouth, "Easy now. Easy."

Ma waddled back to her pie, saying, "Take a look at them steaks in about five minutes, Ann. They're almost ready."

Ann bit her lip, then she said, "I'm grateful to you for getting me this job, but it's kind of hard on my temper. What I've been trying to tell you is that these men start drinking right after breakfast, so by the time they get in here for their dinner, their tongues are pretty loose. They've been talking tough, about the crooked draw and how you won't do anything about it, so they're going to lynch you and Mandell and Ryan. They seem to class all three of you together. I don't know why."

"I don't, either," Johnny said bitterly. "It doesn't make a lick of sense, but I know that's the way most of them feel. I guess it's mostly because I jailed your pa, and maybe partly because I've got to defend the company's right to dispose of its land and I can't just move in and take over the drawing myself which I guess is what they think I ought to do."

She nodded. "I suppose so, but even if these men are not very brave, the whisky will make them think they are. It's not going to take much to start the riot. They'll kill you if you try to stop them, and I don't want that to happen."

"I don't, either," he said, and reached for her hand. "I don't want to rush things, but Ma's right. I . . ."

She drew her hand away, blushing. "I guess I've been too forward. Right now all I want is to get out of this terrible place to some civilized town where I can get a job. It's just that you're too decent to be killed by a bunch of—of—well, I don't know what to call them."

"I know what you mean," he said, thinking that she hesitated to use the proper word because she would be using it to apply to her father. "I don't know what to call them, either, but I haven't met many of them I like or respect, including Chuck O'Leary." He paused, then asked, "Do you know Norman Bradford?"

She nodded. "That is, I know who he is. He's stopped at our wagon a couple of times and talked. He has a nice wife and a little girl who's precious. Why?"

"I finally got it out of O'Leary that Bradford was the man behind this talk about a crooked draw," Johnny said. "He didn't make it that plain, but Bradford admitted it when I talked to him. What I started to say is that Bradford is different from these other men. He struck me as being a pretty solid citizen."

She nodded. "I thought so, too. Well, why did he start the talk about a crooked draw?"

He told her what Bradford had said about Ryan and Babs. Suddenly Ma bellowed, "What the hell, Ann! I told you to watch that steak, but no, you've been sitting there gabbing and let it burn till it ain't fit for hogs to eat."

Ann ran to the stove and forked the meat from the frying pan onto the plates Ma had set out for her and Johnny. "No, the meat's all right," Ann said. A moment later she brought the plates and sat down beside Johnny again. She whispered, "I'm sorry, but I just about ruined the meat. It isn't very good, but please try to eat it."

She wouldn't look at him. He said, "Sure, I can eat it."

He did, although it was so dried out and hard that it was about like eating leather. A few more seconds on the stove and it would have been ruined completely. Later Ann brought him a wide slab of pie and filled his coffee cup again. She didn't return to sit beside him, but remained on the other side of the counter. When he patted the bench beside him, she shook her head.

"I'll stay over here," she said. "You'll think I'm not a good cook, but I really am. I just had to tell you about the talk I've been hearing all afternoon. They say Plug Tully's toughs can't stop them. They'll hang Tully, too if he gets in the way. His men along with him if they have to." She hesitated, her eyes searching Johnny's face, then she said, "I guess it wouldn't be any use to ask you to leave camp."

He shook his head. "No, I'm stuck here. You wouldn't have any use for me if I ran. I'm scared, all right, but I've got to stay and do what I can. I think these fellows are more wind than anything else. When it gets down to cases, Bradford is the only one who will stand and fight."

"If he does, the rest of them might," she said. "Or if somebody succeeds in doing what Pa tried to do. It could set the whole thing off."

"It might at that," he said. "Fix a plate for your pa. It's time for his supper, too, I guess."

Ma finished the pie and popped it into the oven. She moved along the counter to stand in front of Johnny. "I guess Ann's been telling you about the hanging talk." He nodded and she went on, "You can't be sure, but it struck me as being mostly wind."

"That's what I just told Ann," Johnny said. "The thing is that sometimes men like these fellows blow up enough wind that they think they've got to make it good."

"Sometimes it works that way," she agreed. "Well, if you need us, just whistle. We've got guns here and I can shoot. Billy can, too." He had come back into the tent with another armload of stove wood. She added loudly, "If he don't want to fight, I'll kick his butt clean across the California line."

Billy straightened up and scowled. He said, "I heard that. Ain't it enough that I work all day? Now I've got to fight all night."

"Maybe that's just what you're gonna have to do," Ma said blandly.

Billy went out, shaking his head. When Dillon's plate and cup of coffee were set on the counter, Johnny paid for the supper he had eaten, then said, "Ma, you keep track of the meals that go to the jail and collect from the county when you get back to Piute."

"I sure figure on doing that," she said.

Johnny picked up the plate and coffee cup and left the tent. Men had gathered along the street in knots, and as he passed, he felt their hard stares, heard their muttered threats, but he didn't look at them or hurry his pace.

As he passed the ranch house, he saw a sweat-gummed horse tied in front. He wondered about it, and as soon as he handed Dillon his supper, he went back to the house and turned up the path from the street. He stopped before he stepped through the doorway and heard Mandell say, "It's a very touchy situation. Most of these men are shiftless drifters. Actually they have nothing to complain about. What's happened is they have finally realized that only one of them is going to get the Cross Heart and they seem to figure it's going to be the other fellow."

"I'll have a talk with them," a man said.

Johnny's heart bounced and then sank. He guessed he'd had a hunch when he'd seen the lathered horse. He couldn't see the man who had spoken, but he knew the voice. It was Ed Neal's.

He strode through the doorway and wheeled to face Neal who sat in a chair tipped back against the wall. He said angrily, "What are you doing here, Ed? Didn't you think I could handle the job?"

Neal motioned toward Ryan and Mandell. "They sent for me."

Johnny whirled to face Ryan. For a moment he fought his soaring temper and lost. He grabbed a fistful of Ryan's shirt and twisted it. "By God," he said between clenched teeth, "I ought to beat you to death. Nothing has happened. Why did you send for the sheriff?"

White-faced, Ryan began to back up as Babs cried, "Don't hit him, Johnny. It was Mandell who sent the wire."

Slowly Johnny released his grip on Ryan's shirt and turned to Mandell. He said, "If it wasn't for your white hair, I'd show you how big a mistake you made. What excuse have you got for sending for the sheriff?"

"Just one," Mandell didn't back up or indicate in any way that he was scared. "Or rather, I should say there are five hundred. They've been drinking all day, and they've been told lies and they're getting uglier all the time. I saw this coming last night and I knew we had to do something."

He glanced at Neal and then brought his gaze back to Johnny. "I've got nothing against you, Lund, but I know this job is going to take more than one man. The sheriff's older and more experienced than you are. The men will be more likely to listen to a sheriff than a deputy. I did you a favor, but I doubt that you've got sense enough to see it."

"Don't do me any more favors," Johnny said. "Come on, Ed. I've got some things to tell you they'll never get around to saying. Ryan, take care of the sheriff's horse."

Neal rose. "I haven't et yet. Don't Ma Ketchum have a cafe here?"

"Yeah, we'll go see her." Johnny looked at Ryan who had been insulted at being considered a hostler who had nothing to do but take care of Neal's horse. "You heard what I said, Ryan. All I need to muss up that purty face of yours is an excuse. If you don't feed and rub that animal down, I'll work you over till Babs won't recognize you."

Ryan swallowed and said sullenly, "He'll be taken care of."

As soon as Neal and Johnny were out of the house, Neal said, “You’ve been eating nothing but raw meat since you came here. I never heard you talk to a man like you just talked to Ryan.”

“You bet I’ve been eating raw meat,” Johnny said. “Chauncey Ryan is enough to make any man eat raw meat.”

“He’s got a purty daughter,” Neal said. “Don’t that help?”

“Daughter, hell,” Johnny said. “She’s no more his daughter than I am. She’s his woman. I’ll tell you about it while you eat.”

CHAPTER XV

Johnny stopped when they reached the street and faced Neal. He said, "You made it mighty plain when you sent me down here that it was my show and I was to handle it. Am I fired?"

"Hell no," Neal said, surprised. "If it'll make you feel any better, I'll tell you I was wrong to send you. I should have come myself. I had no idea the drawing was a trick or would attract so many men."

Johnny turned toward Ma's Kitchen, relieved in one way. In another he wasn't relieved at all. He would just as soon have saddled his horse and ridden out of Mallard City. It was a mess and he had a feeling that both the company and the settlers deserved whatever happened to them.

Now, as he strode along the street with Neal, he saw that more men had gathered between the company office and Ma's Kitchen than there had been a few minutes before when he had taken Dillon's supper to him. He felt their hatred pushing at him and Neal; he heard some of their threats and insults, muttered at first, then distinct and clear.

"There's the old he-coon himself from Piute City. Look at him strut with that tin star on his shirt."

"Looks like he didn't figure the cub could take care of things down here."

"Let's rip that star off him. He won't be strutting so good then."

At first Neal paid no attention, then he turned his head to look at Johnny. He said in a low tone, "I've never heard anything like this. What's the matter with these guys? Most of 'em never seen me before. Do they think we're gonna steal the Cross Heart?"

"It's just because we're the law," Johnny said, "and they figure the law is on the side of the company and the company is cheating 'em."

"Let's run a few of these loud talkers in," Neal said. "No reason we should take this kind of abuse. You got any room in your jail?"

Johnny shook his head. "Not for them. Ignore 'em. I arrested Dillon last night for trying to murder Ryan. That's what started the trouble. If we take any of these men in, we'll bring on a ringtailed wowser of a riot. There's probably a hundred men or more on this street."

"They need to learn something about talking to a lawman," Neal said stubbornly.

"Let's get your supper first," Johnny said. "Here's Ma's place."

Johnny motioned for Neal to go in first, then he followed. Ed Neal was a strange one, he thought. There was no doubt about the sheriff's gut courage. He would have taken the mob on single handed, yet it was common gossip in Piute that his wife gave the orders at home and Ed Neal took them the way any hen-pecked husband did. All it proved, Johnny thought, was the single fact that you never knew how courage was going to run in a man.

A few settlers were eating supper. Neal went on around the corner to an open place on the counter and called, "How's business, Ma?"

She wheeled away from the stove, saw who it was, and squealed, "Ed, you long-horned, old star toter! What are you doing down here? Johnny send for you?"

"No," Neal said as he shook hands. "I just thought I'd look things over. I'm hungry, too."

"What'll you have? Steak?"

"What else have you got?"

"Steak."

"I'll have steak."

Ma bellowed a great laugh. "You ain't changed, Ed. Not one bit. Ann, meet the sheriff, Ed Neal. Sheriff, meet my waitress, Ann Dillon. She just came to work this morning and she's a dandy."

Ann offered her hand, saying, "I'm pleased to meet you, Mr. Neal. I'm glad Ma thinks I'm a good one because she's been cracking the whip ever since Johnny brought me here."

Ma snorted. "Don't waste none of your sympathy on her, Ed, and don't let that young whipper-snapper of a deputy get close to her or they'll start holding hands and then you won't get no service and your steak will be burned."

Ann turned her back on Neal and said nothing. Ma drifted off to cut the pie she had just taken out of the oven. Neal asked in a low tone, "Is she any relation to the man you jailed for trying to kill Ryan?"

Johnny nodded. "His daughter, but she's not like him. She's a fine young woman. I like her."

Neal shot him a suspicious glance. "You sweet on her like Ma says?"

"I haven't known her long enough to be sure," Johnny said. "I always figured love at first sight was a bunch of hogwash, but now I dunno. I just never met a girl like her before."

"Well, don't let her talk you into getting married," Neal grunted. "That's one penal institution where you automatically get a life sentence. All right, now tell me what's going on. I figured I wasn't getting the straight of it from Mandell and Ryan."

Johnny told him what had happened. Ann brought his dinner and Neal ate as Johnny talked. He ended with, "Plug Tully's toughs can't be counted on for any help. They tried to take Dillon away from me after the shooting, saying they were going to hang him. They had odds of six to one, but they didn't get him."

Neal nodded, grinning as he picked up his coffee cup. "It's like I said, son. You've been eating raw meat since you came down here."

"Naw." Johnny shook his head. "I just don't think Tully and his crowd have got the guts it takes to give Ryan and Mandell the protection they need, not when it comes to facing five hundred men who are mad enough and drunk enough to be ugly."

"You figure this Bradford can help? Or maybe the question is, will he help?"

"We've got to figure on it," Johnny said. "He's a solid man, and I believe his story about Ryan and Babs. The only thing I keep wondering about is whether he's got some kind of an ax to grind by spreading the story about a crooked draw. He claims he don't want a riot, neither, but he knows that's exactly what's going to happen if we don't think of something, and he knows he's responsible for it."

"This attitude of honesty and innocence you say he has is the best disguise in the world," Neal said. "I'd say it's a safe bet he's got his private little scheme."

"But I can't see . . ." Johnny stopped and slapped himself on the forehead. "Why hell, it's as plain as the big nose on my face. I don't know why I didn't think of it before. If Bradford gets a delay in the drawing, these men who have bought tickets will be starving and wanting to move on. Most of 'em don't have much money, and they'll soon eat up what they do have. A delay might last for weeks before new men got here to run the drawing."

"Why, I think you've hit it," Neal said. "They'll sell their tickets for ten cents on the dollar or whatever Bradford will pay and they'll move on. When the drawing actually takes place, Bradford will be sitting here by himself with all the tickets, or most of them, so he's bound to get something, the timber land if not the Cross Heart."

"And for a fraction of what it would have cost him if he had bought the tickets from the company." Johnny shook his head in disgust. "I should have thought of that a long time ago, but I guess he fooled me with his honest face."

"A good actor can fool any of us," Neal said. Ann brought his piece of pie, and as she turned away, he said, "Miss Dillon, you've had a lot of these men in here today. What do you think of them? I mean, their temper or feelings?"

"They're mad," she said. "It's more than being angry. They've been drinking until they're dangerous. I suppose they've been egged on by somebody, probably Norman Bradford. I told Johnny he ought to ride out of here. There isn't any sense in getting killed helping protect a company like this." She shrugged. "But I guess he won't do it."

"Believe me, Miss Dillon," Neal said, "that's exactly what I'd like to do, but I won't do it, either."

"I know," she said, "but one side's as bad as the other, and that includes my own father. I guess it's kind of like being outside in a storm and you see a lightning flash coming right at you, but you just stand there and let it hit you."

"That's about the size of it," Neal agreed.

She turned back to the stove. Neal finished his pie and shoved his plate back. As he reached for his coffee cup, he asked, "You got any ideas?"

"One," Johnny said, "just one. It sure ain't original, but it might satisfy the settlers even if it does play Bradford's game for him. I think we've got to wire the company office and ask them to send new men out here and postpone the drawing till they get here."

Neal nodded. "I was thinking the same. We can't help it if we're playing Bradford's game. Our job is to keep order and we can't do that if a riot starts. If Bradford's right, I don't have any sympathy for the company."

"Neither have I," Johnny agreed. "We know they lied time after time when they sold the tickets. If they're crooked enough to do that, they're crooked enough to hold a dishonest drawing."

Neal rose and dropped a coin on the counter as he called, "Ma." She had been washing dishes at her work table. Now she came toward him, wiping her hands on her apron.

"I didn't have no notion about what was going

on till I got here," Neal said, "but now I've heard Ryan and Mandell, I've heard Johnny's story, and I've heard Miss Dillon say the settlers are mad. Ma, I know you're a hard-headed woman who don't scare easy. How does it stack up to you?"

She glanced at the men who were sitting at the front side of the counter, then she leaned forward and whispered. "I'm scared now, Ed. I'd sure hate to have this place wrecked. It's all I've got. If we get a riot, that's what will happen. Men quit being men. They don't reason. They turn into animals and the rioting is like a disease. It spreads."

Neal nodded. "I guess you're in the best position of anybody in camp to know what the feeling is."

"I figure I am," she agreed. "I've heard it all afternoon. Take any one of these men and you've got a coward on your hands. Put five hundred of 'em together and you've got a sore-tailed grizzly who'd have this camp torn apart before midnight."

"Come on, Johnny," Neal said. "Let's go find that telegraph office."

CHAPTER XVI

Ed Neal chewed on the end of a pencil as he stood at the crude desk in the telegraph office, his eyes on the wall in front of him. Finally he said, "Hell, Johnny, this ain't no time to beat around the bush. I'll just tell 'em straight out that they've got to recall Ryan and Mandell and send out two new men. It's either that or riot, which same would be a disaster to 'em. A riot will end with a lot of bad publicity and destruction, and Ryan and Mandell lynched to boot."

"That's right," Johnny agreed. "Yeah, that's all you need to say, except maybe that the settlers have lost confidence in Mandell and Ryan. If they tear the place apart, it'll be the company's fault, not ours."

"Yeah," Neal grunted, "but it won't be any help to you'n me whether the company's at fault or not."

"If there's a riot, we're dead ducks," Johnny said. "That it?"

"That's it," Neal said.

He wrote laboriously for a time, then handed the paper to Johnny who read it and nodded. "Good," he said. "Get it on the wire."

Neal took the paper from him and gave it to the telegrapher who read it and said, "It'll go out right away, Sheriff. Chances are you'll have an answer in a few hours. Stop in first thing in the morning."

"I'll do that," Neal said, and left the office, Johnny following.

The street was nearly deserted, and Neal asked about it. "They light out for the platform where the drawing's held and stand around and visit," Johnny said. "We'd better have our talk with Ryan and Mandell and get over there. The sooner we tell the settlers what we've done, the better."

"I reckon so," Neal agreed. "Mandell and Ryan will raise hell and no mistake, but I don't see any other way out of it." He took a cigar from his pocket and bit off the end, then fished a match out of his pocket and fired the cigar. He said, "Johnny, I ain't sure we've got the authority to do this."

"We haven't done anything, Ed," Johnny said. "Not yet anyway. We simply asked the company to do something which seems reasonable under the circumstances. If the company won't do it, we'll have to go along. If it does, it's their responsibility. Either way, the company's responsible for what happens."

"I know, I know," Neal said. "It's just that I never faced a situation like this before and it's hard to know for sure what's the right thing to do. I guess I have the feeling that we ought to go ahead as planned and it's up to us to keep order."

"You'll change your mind when you face the crowd," Johnny said. "About keeping order, I mean."

It was twilight now, the lamps and lanterns in the ranch house and tents along the street coming to life. As Neal turned toward the front door of the ranch house, he said, "We tell Ryan and Mandell, then we tell the crowd. If the company refuses to send new men, I suppose they'll go ahead with the drawing tomorrow."

"I'm sure they will," Johnny said, "and we can't stop them."

Mandell and Ryan were talking when Neal and Johnny came in. Babs was halfway down the stairs. She kept coming until she reached the bottom step, then stopped, her gaze on Neal as if waiting to hear the bad news. Mandell and Ryan stopped talking. Like Babs, Johnny thought, they must have sensed that something had happened, so they waited.

"You people will not go ahead with the drawing tonight," Neal said.

"Oh, we won't, will we?" Ryan asked sharply. "Now just who the hell do you think you are to give us that kind of an order. Maybe you'll throw us into jail because you don't like the way we comb our hair."

"We'll throw you into jail if we have to, but it won't be for the way you comb your hair," Neal said. "It'll be for your safety. Johnny says we're close to having a riot. You thought so, too, or you wouldn't have sent for me. We cannot guarantee your safety if it happens."

"You think tomorrow night's going to be any different?" Ryan demanded.

"No, I don't," Neal said, "but we figure that a delay for several days or weeks will give the settlers a chance to cool off."

"You're crazy," Ryan said angrily. "We won't stop the drawing for weeks or even days."

"I'm hoping you won't have any say about it." Neal's cigar had gone cold and he lighted it again. "We just wired the company that the settlers have no confidence in you men and we asked them to recall you two and send a new crew to take charge of the drawing."

Mandell didn't say a word and he didn't move. As far as Johnny could tell, he wasn't worried in the least. His expression didn't change except for a tight grin that touched the corners of his mouth. Babs' lips parted in shocked surprise and then she became angry. She started to swear, then stopped, her gaze turning to Ryan.

"Chauncey," Babs said. "You'd better tell these two star-toters they can't do this to us."

Ryan was the one Johnny expected trouble from, so after a quick glance at Mandell and Babs, he gave the man his complete attention, his right hand wrapped around the butt of his gun.

He said, "Ryan, if you start anything, you're a dead man."

"I ain't starting a thing," Ryan said. "You're the ones who are starting something. I guess I'd better call Plug Tully and his men in here. You two bastards don't throw half as long a shadow as you think you do."

"Maybe we will have to throw you into jail," Neal said, "and the way you comb your hair might be as good an excuse as any. I don't want any trouble with your gunslingers. All I've got to say is that you will not have a drawing tonight. If the company refuses our request, you can go ahead tomorrow. If it agrees to send out new men, I want all three of you out of camp before tomorrow night."

For a moment Ryan's rebellious gaze wavered, his right hand moving toward the butt of his gun. He was having trouble making up his mind, Johnny thought. It went against his grain to back up, but he was a reasonably intelligent and cautious man, and it would certainly be a fool act to draw on two men when he had no idea how fast they were.

He was furious. It showed in the color of his face, in the nervous twitching of his lips, in his eyes, and Johnny would not have been surprised if he elected to go for his gun. But he didn't. His hand fell away from the butt of his gun.

"By God," Ryan said, "I'll tell you one thing

that you'd better not forget. If you get me throwed out of my job because of some gossip that's been spreading through the crowd, I'll kill you. Both of you, and I'll sue the company for breach of contract."

"You'd better cool down, Ryan," Neal said hotly, "or I'll throw you into jail for our protection. I don't like to hear a man threaten to kill me. He might really try it."

Plug Tully appeared in the doorway, two of his men standing behind him. He said, "The torches are lighted, Mr. Mandell. You want us to move the stuff to the platform now?"

"No," Mandell said. "We're not having the drawing tonight." He looked at Neal. "Just what do you think will happen when Ryan and Babs fail to show up over there?"

"We're going to tell the crowd what's happened," Neal said. "There won't be any trouble. Not tonight."

"Very well," Mandell said. "It's your party. Go ahead and enjoy yourself." He winked at Ryan who had turned sullen, his brooding eyes on Neal. "Don't get boogery, Chauncey. Our lawmen have made jackasses out of themselves. It was our mistake sending for the sheriff. I think it's a fair guess that young Lund would not have tried a fool play like this."

Neal muttered something and turned toward the door. Johnny said, "Wait, Ed. I'd like to know why Mandell is so sure of his position."

"I'll be glad to tell you," Mandell said, smiling smugly. "Why do you think I was sent here?"

"I've sure wondered," Johnny said.

"I can tell you in a few words," Mandell said. "I am the company. Or part of it anyway. The other owners who bought the wagon road grant with me are my friends. They trust me and they will never in the world agree to what you're asking because they do trust me. None of the others wanted to come out here to this empty, God-forsaken country to supervise the drawing. They also trust Ryan or they would not have hired him. All you have done is to make us lose one night's drawing, but we can catch up tomorrow night."

"Come on, Johnny," Neal said. "We'd better get over there."

Johnny stared at Mandell, wondering if he was telling the truth. He wheeled and left the room, catching up with Neal before he reached the street. He asked, "How did it strike you, Ryan threatening to kill us if we got him thrown out of his job?"

"He proved one thing to me," Neal said. "He was too worried. This job ain't worth it. I'm guessing your Norman Bradford was right about him being a crook. He's playing his own game and we're keeping him from finishing it if we make him lose his job. That's the way I sized it up." Neal took several steps, then said, "It must be a big deal for him to threaten us that way. If you get shot, he's the first one I'd look for after hearing him make that threat."

"That's just what I was thinking," Johnny said. "If the company insists on Ryan going ahead with the drawing, we'll have trouble with the settlers, and if the company don't, we can figure on Ryan trying to murder us."

"A pleasant prospect," Neal said.

A moment later they reached the platform, the torches throwing their weird, flickering light all around just as they had last night, but Johnny had an entirely different feeling now. They had brought a reprieve. No more. But at least there would be no trouble until they heard from the company.

If Mandell was right and the company refused to go along with Neal's request, tomorrow night would be like last night, only worse. Johnny was as sure as he could be that the explosion would come soon if the drawing continued under Ryan.

Neal stood near the front edge of the platform and raised a hand for silence. Johnny, to one side and a little behind him, stared at the sea of faces. He could distinguish the ones in front clearly, but farther back and on the sides the light was too dim for him to make them out.

He had a scarey feeling that there were thousands of them out there, enemies, hostile men and women. They were silent, their faces turned toward the platform. Again, as he had so many times today, he felt the wave of hatred from them that pushed at him. They would hang him if they could, just as they would hang Ryan and Mandell. They felt the same way about Ed Neal. Like Johnny, he was the law, and the company owned the law.

They had come to that conclusion and they would hold to it unless something happened to give them a different attitude. They were no longer reasoning human beings; they were predatory animals running in a great pack as they waited to pull down their prey. Somehow it seemed unreal to Johnny, yet he could not shake off the feeling that violence was a time bomb, with the time almost run out.

"I'm Ed Neal, the county sheriff," Neal said. "I understand from my deputy and other people I have talked to that most of you are dissatisfied with the manner in which the drawing is being held. For that reason we have wired the company asking them for a delay and to recall the men who are conducting the drawing. We have no power to force the company to accept this suggestion, but we hope they will. If you will return here at this same time tomorrow night, we will give you the company's decision."

Finished, Neal turned and walked off the platform, Johnny a step behind him. The settlers didn't move for a time, apparently dazed by the news that they were getting what they wanted. At least the law had asked the company to do it, and that was more than they had expected. Now, Johnny thought, maybe they won't think we're as bad as the company men.

Neal stopped at the edge of the platform and wiped his face with his bandanna. "My God, I never went through anything like that before," he said. "You were right, Johnny, about me changing my mind when I faced the crowd. We couldn't begin to keep order if that bunch went crazy. I kept feeling they were just waiting for a chance to put a rope around my neck. But why? They don't have any reason to hate me."

"They don't have any reason to hate me, either," Johnny said, "but that's the way it's been all day. I think that almost every man out there feels the way Al Dillon did last night. If their ticket is a loser as his was, any of them might do exactly what he tried to do. But now there's a difference as far as you and me are concerned. They'll have to figure we're on their side."

"But it don't change the way they feel toward Mandell and Ryan," Neal said. "We can't let 'em hang those men, but I'm not sure we can stop 'em."

The crowd was beginning to scatter, still silent. Norman Bradford came around the front of the platform and shook hands with Neal as he introduced himself. "I want to thank you for what you did tonight," Bradford said. "I made it plain to your deputy the way I feel about Ryan and the woman. We all think that any change the company makes will be for the better."

"You understand that we cannot guarantee any change," Neal said. "What will happen if there ain't?"

"I can't tell," Bradford answered. "Let's hope the company has some sense. There'll be hell to pay if they keep Ryan and Mandell on the job."

He nodded pleasantly and strode away toward his wagon. Neal said softly, "Well, you were right about him, Johnny. He's a very honest man, and he could not possibly have a selfish motive."

Johnny grinned. "I'm glad you agree."

"And that's the kind of man you had better watch out for," Neal said. "Now I'm going to find me a bed."

He disappeared into the darkness. Johnny waited until the last of the crowd had left, then he walked away. He wondered if Ma Ketchum had let Ann go yet. He decided to find out.

CHAPTER XVII

Tebo Rand did not leave his wagon from the time he'd had the fight with Johnny Lund until evening. All he wanted to do was nurse his bruises and hurts.

Lund had hurt him more than physically. The kid deputy had made him look bad, and the fact that he'd taken the beating in front of the girl he had just asked to marry him made it all the worse. He guessed he hadn't landed a single blow.

So he sat in the shade of his wagon and smoked and whittled, or just sat. When anyone went by and spoke to him, he answered in surly monosyllables. He had not made any friends in camp, so now none of his neighbors made the slightest effort to find out what was wrong. He let them know he wanted to be let alone, and they were willing to oblige.

He gave considerable thought to squaring the account with Lund. Not Ann Dillon, because he was perfectly willing to forget her. More than one woman had humiliated him in his lifetime; he had made it a guiding principle to never let any woman humiliate him more than once, so he simply put Ann out of his thoughts. Johnny Lund was another matter.

Rand remembered he had talked big about

using his gun the next time they met, but now that he had time to think about it, he knew he would never take that kind of a chance. At least not in a fair, face-to-face duel. If Johnny Lund was too fast for him with his fists, the odds were he'd be too fast with a gun, and a gun was a final way to end an argument, too final when he had a big chance of losing.

He was not a gambler when the odds were against him. He wasn't even a gambler when they were even. That left him with only one choice. He could shoot Lund in the back. It probably wouldn't be hard to find the opportunity if he waited in the darkness around the jail.

The more he thought about it, the more he wanted to do it. Lund's murder would bring the sheriff in from Piute, but that didn't mean anything. The sheriff would have no reason to nail him for the killing. It could be any of the five hundred men in camp. Now he was in a hell of indecision, caught between his desire to kill young Lund and the fear that the killing might backfire. He still had not made up his mind by the time he ate supper.

When it was dusk, the settlers began moving toward the platform. Rand went along out of curiosity as much as anything. He wouldn't get the Cross Heart until near the end of the draw, probably on Sunday, so he had to wait. The only worry he had was that another hothead like Al

Dillon would make another try. If Ryan was shot, Tebo Rand's whole scheme went up in smoke. He would never get to another man the way he had Ryan.

He was surprised that the wheel of fortune and the map of the wagon road grant were not on the platform. Neither Ryan nor Babs were in sight. He wondered about that, too. It was not like Ryan to be slow getting the drawing started.

There was a good deal of grumbling from the crowd because Ryan had not appeared, then Rand saw Johnny Lund and an older man mount the platform. He had never seen the older man before, but he wore a star, too, so Rand assumed he was the sheriff, an assumption that was confirmed as soon as Ed Neal began to speak.

The longer Neal talked, the more frantic Rand became. He didn't need to worry about Ryan being shot. Neal and Lund were trying to get Ryan fired. As far as Tebo Rand's plans were concerned, it added up to the same thing.

The moment that Neal finished talking, Rand ran toward the company headquarters. He didn't know what Ryan could do, but he had to see the man. There must be something. This deal couldn't go down the drain now.

Always before when he had wanted to see Ryan, he had waited outside in the darkness until he found a way to attract the man's attention. Ryan would leave the house and they would talk in the cover of darkness. This time he was in no mood to be careful. He simply ran up the path from the street, opened the door, and went into the house, not giving a thought about anyone seeing him.

Ryan sat at his desk smoking a cigar, a pile of papers in front of him, but Rand had the impression the man was not working. He was canted back in his swivel chair, a cigar tucked into one corner of his mouth, his eyes on the ceiling. Babs sat in a chair a few feet from Ryan, some sewing on her lap. She didn't appear to be working on it any more than Ryan was working on his pile of papers.

Ryan sat straight up with a jerk the instant Rand came through the door. When he saw who it was, he yanked the cigar out of his mouth, his face turning red with fury. "What the hell are you doing here? You know better than to—"

"Shut up," Rand said. "I had to talk to you. I just came from where you and Babs should have been taking care of tonight's drawing, but a couple of lawmen were there instead. The sheriff made his pitch about wiring the company and wanting you and Mandell removed. Is that true?"

Ryan shrugged. "As far as I know it is. He came in here with the same story. I didn't see him send the wire if that's what you mean."

Rand looked around. "Where's Mandell?"

"I don't run herd on the old man," Ryan said

harshly. "Why don't you go back to your camp and wait? There's nothing we can do until we hear from the company. We will first thing in the morning. If I'm fired, our deal's off. It's that simple."

"It can't be." Rand grabbed Ryan by the shoulders and shook him. "You've got to do something."

Ryan jerked free and stood up. "Keep your hands off me, Rand. Babs and me want to go through with our agreement as bad as you do, and we will if we can. That's all I can tell you."

"That's not enough." Rand moistened dry lips and looked at Babs. "What about it? You can tell me more than Ryan's telling me, can't you? I just don't believe this deal is going to slip right through our fingers when we're this close to winding it up."

She gave him her tantalizing smile and winked. "I don't know, Tebo. We wait. That's all."

She was the most sensual woman he had ever seen. Whenever she looked at him that way, he wanted her more than he had ever wanted a woman before in his life. She probably affected every man the same way, but he had never attempted to move in. Chauncey Ryan would kill if he tried. He had no doubt of that whatever.

"I've been able to wait," Rand said slowly, "figuring it was just a matter of getting most of the drawing out of the way to satisfy the company and maybe sell a few more tickets." Rand sucked in a long breath and shook his head. "But this is different. What are the chances the company will do it?"

Ryan walked away from his desk to a window. He glanced at Babs, took the cigar out of his mouth, and flicked off the ash, then put the cigar back between his teeth. He said, "Personally I don't know. Mandell is the only company man I've known well enough to make any kind of judgment about, but Mandell claims he's not worried at all. He laughed at the sheriff and said he was the company, or part of it anyway, and none of the other owners wanted to come out here. If he's right, we have nothing to worry about."

Babs had kept on smiling at him, her eyes inviting him as plainly as a woman could without using words. She said, "You see, Tebo. We wait. We just have to wait."

Rand turned and strode out of the room. He had to. He heard them talking behind him, he heard Babs' soft laugh, and was filled with a wild and sudden rage. She was practicing on him, he thought. She hadn't meant any of it. He had a feeling she had humiliated him without appearing to or saying anything, and now they were laughing at him.

He stopped in the darkness in front of the house, hating Ryan and Babs, and having to fight an impulse to go back and shoot Ryan and beat Babs until she was nothing more than a piece of jellied flesh. He had never had a worse day than this one.

Suddenly he realized he was breathing hard and his fists were clenched so hard they hurt. No, it wasn't worth it. Not when there was a chance he could make the deal for the Cross Heart. Mandell might be right.

He started back to his wagon, then remembered that he had thought seriously of dry-gulching Johnny Lund. That was something else that must be put off. Now that the sheriff was here in camp, there was no sense in letting a desire for personal revenge get in the way of gaining a bigger goal.

Rand's hunger to own the Cross Heart had become so great that it was a consuming fire. Nothing else really mattered. Maybe later, once he had the ranch, he could take care of both Chauncey Ryan and Johnny Lund, but it would have to wait.

CHAPTER XVIII

When Johnny stepped into Ma's Kitchen, he saw that Ma and Ann were finishing the dishes. Billy Bean was not in sight. Ma said, "If you're hungry, bucko, you came to the wrong place. We're done cooking for today."

She sounded tired and Johnny thought she had a right to be, going as hard as she had since early morning. Ann smiled at him, a smile that seemed almost as tired as Ma's voice.

"I never in my life saw two women who were as beat as you two sound and look," Johnny said.

"You ain't far wrong," Ma answered. "We're just as beat as we sound and look." She straightened and put a hand to her back. "I dunno if I can go another day like this or not. I like to make money, but I don't cotton to lose ten years of my life doing it."

"You hear what happened tonight?" Johnny asked.

"No," Ma said. "I've been wondering. Nobody's been in here since the drawing."

"There was no drawing," Johnny said, and told them about the telegram that Neal had sent the company office and their talk with Mandell and Ryan. "It didn't take long to tell the settlers about the postponement, but it's hard to figure what will happen now, especially if the company says to go ahead, which is what Mandell says they'll do."

"Mandell's probably right, too," Ma said. "He's a smart old coot."

Ann finished drying the dishes and hung her dishcloth on a cord that had been stretched back of the stove. She said, "Johnny, the settlers are like a bunch of kids. They think they know what they want, but they really don't. You see, they can't stay here for weeks if it takes that long to get new men out here, and it probably will because the company doesn't care. They've got more tickets to sell, and they'll welcome the chance to sell the rest of them."

"So what will the settlers do if they can't stay here?" Johnny asked.

"They'll drift on," she said sourly. "That's what most of them have been doing all their lives, including Al and Ann Dillon."

Ma gave the girl a sharp look, and said, "Johnny came in to spark me, but he can't do it with you standing there, so you go on to bed."

Ann laughed in spite of herself. "All right, Ma. I sure don't want to get in the way of Johnny's sparking."

"Would it hurt your feelings, Ma," Johnny said, "if I came right out and told you I came in to spark Ann?"

"Oh, it sure would," Ma said, feigning anger.

"All right, if that's the way you feel, get out of here, both of you."

Johnny grinned as he moved around the counter to the back. Ann met him, and they left the tent together, Johnny saying, "I guess Ma ain't so bad off, joshing us that way."

"No," Ann agreed. "She couldn't be."

They walked to the Dillon wagon, Johnny saying, "I won't keep you up late." When he reached for her hand, she did not pull it away. He added, "I'll wait until you haven't worked so hard to get to the serious business of sparking."

For a moment she didn't say anything. She stood beside him, her hand gripped by his, her shoulder touching his. Finally she said, "I guess I've thanked you for getting me this job, but I want to thank you again. I don't know what I would have done if you hadn't got it for me. Ma's promised me five dollars a day. I've seen the time I was glad to work for five dollars a week. I'm putting in long hours and working hard, but I like it. I suppose it won't last long."

"No, I doubt that it will last past the end of the week," Johnny said. "What will you do then?"

"I don't know," she said miserably. "I just don't know."

She was thinking of her father, Johnny knew, and it was a shame she was bound to him. Actually there was no reason she should be. He could making a living if he would, and if he did, she would be able to make her own way.

"Ann," he said, "you can't spend your life looking out for your father."

"I know that," she said. "He's healthy enough and strong enough to hold down a job, but he never has. Not for long anyhow. The world's against him, he says. What can I do about him, Johnny?"

"You can let him starve," he answered. "That would be one way to make him go to work. As long as you make a living for him, he'll go on just the way he is."

"I suppose so," she said. "But I can't stand to see him go hungry. Ma was that way, too. She worked herself to death supporting him."

"For a while you won't have any worry," he said. "Your pa will be in jail until his trial. If he's convicted of attempted murder, he'll be in jail for quite a while. I'd like to see you come to Piute. Ma will probably go back and start her cafe again. She'll give you a job. If she doesn't, I think I can get work for you in the hotel. Neither one would be good jobs, but you'd have a living."

For a minute she didn't say anything, then he heard a sound that might have been a sob. "Oh, Johnny, you don't know how much you've done for me today." She kissed him quickly on the cheek and turned and stepped into the wagon, calling back, "Good night."

He walked around the tent to the street, wondering as he had several times today how a man like Al Dillon could have fathered a girl like Ann. When he reached the jail, he unlocked the door and called, "Dillon."

The man shambled out of the dark interior of the building, saying, "That's a hell of a hole you're keeping me penned up in. If you're gonna hold me in jail, how about taking me to Piute where you've got a regular jail."

"Oh, you'd love it," Johnny said sarcastically. "Sorry, Dillon. I can't leave."

"Start me toward Piute," Dillon urged. "I'd get there after a while."

"If I put you on a horse and headed you for Piute," Johnny said, "you'd go there and lock yourself in the jail, I suppose."

"Sure I would," Dillon said.

"Let me tell you something about yourself," Johnny said. "You're old enough to be my father, but there's no dignity to you no matter what your age is, so I'm going to insult you by telling you the truth. You are not only a shiftless and lazy drifter who has lived off women all your life. You're also a liar. You wouldn't go five miles in Piute's direction. You'd steal the horse and head for the California line."

Dillon didn't say anything for a long moment. He was breathing hard. Johnny thought he felt insulted if he could be insulted. Maybe he had never been talked to that way before, but Johnny doubted that words could change the man or reach him in any way.

Finally Dillon asked, "What do you mean about living off women?"

"I just left Ann," Johnny answered. "She's a fine woman. She's worked for Ma Ketchum today until she's so tired she's ready to drop. She's worried about you and what will happen to you if and when you get out of jail. She's worried about herself, too. I told her I could probably get a job for her in Piute. I told her that if she'd let you starve, you'd go to work like a man, but she doesn't think she could stand it. She said her ma was the same way, and that her ma had worked herself to death supporting you."

"Ann said that?" Dillon asked incredulously.

"She sure did," Johnny said. "I haven't known her very long, but I aim to get better acquainted with her. I might ask her to marry me except for one thing. I'll never support a lazy father-in-law like you."

Dillon grabbed his arm. "Listen, Lund. I'll make you a promise right now. If you marry Ann, I'll go away. You'll never see me again. I won't be no burden to you. All I want is to know Ann has a home and is being taken care of."

"Get back inside," Johnny ordered. "I'm going to bed."

"You believe me, don't you?" Dillon pressed.

"You will go on seeing Ann, won't you? She's a good girl, a real good girl."

"I know that," Johnny said irritably, "and I'll go on seeing her if she'll see me, but as far as believing you is concerned, I don't, and your promise ain't worth a dime."

Dillon stood in the doorway, peering at Johnny in the darkness. Johnny shoved him inside the building, pulled the door shut and snapped the padlock. As he turned toward his tent, he had the feeling he was trapped. If he married Ann, he'd get her father in spite of all he and Ann could do; in spite of all the promises the man made.

CHAPTER XIX

Chauncey Ryan sat up late for the very good reason that he knew he could not sleep if he went to bed. He had made the agreement with Tebo Rand because he didn't see where it could go wrong. During his lifetime he had made a great deal of money and had lost most of it; he had lived dangerously as he had worked all kinds of con games. Now that he had hooked up with Babs, he had decided it was time to live a safer, less spectacular life. The money he was to receive from Rand was to be the means of attaining that life.

Now, if Ed Neal and Johnny Lund had their way, he'd never get the money from Rand, so he and Babs would have to go on living the same tawdry, dangerous life they had lived for several years, always on the move, always looking back over their shoulders to see if one of their victims was catching up with them.

Even after he went to bed, he still could not sleep, but lay staring into the darkness trying to think of something he could do. As Tebo Rand had said, there must be a way. You just don't give up a proposition as good as this one when you're so close to the finish.

Ryan remembered what George Mandell had

said, that the company would say to go ahead and ignore the sheriff's warning, that he was part of the company and none of the other owners wanted to come out here to Mallard City. At times Mandell had shown some courage, but Ryan had no respect for him, and he didn't believe a man he didn't respect, so he took no stock in what Mandell had said.

When he finally did drop off, he slept so soundly that he did not hear the banging on the front door. Finally Babs couldn't stand it any longer, so she stepped into Ryan's room, lighted a lamp, and shook him awake. She said, "You'd better get downstairs and see who's trying to knock the house down. Maybe it's important."

He yawned and stretched and rubbed his eyes, then blinked owlishly at her until he became aware of the pounding. It still took time to swim up out of the deep pool of sleep and to wipe the cobwebs out of his head. He took the lamp and stumbled down the stairs, finally coming fully awake when he opened the front door and felt the cold rush of night air.

The telegrapher was standing there, a telegram in his hand. He gave the paper to Ryan, saying curtly, "This is for you. I wouldn't have spent ten minutes hammering on your door if I hadn't been ordered to deliver it the minute I got it."

"Thanks, Tom," Ryan said as he took the telegram.

The telegrapher wheeled and disappeared into the darkness. Ryan yawned and kicked the door shut. He climbed the stairs and went back to his room. Babs, sitting on the edge of his bed, asked, "Well, what is it?"

"Just a telegram," Ryan said, and yawned again.

"What's in it?" Babs demanded. "You make me so damned mad sometimes. I suppose you haven't read it?"

"That's right, I haven't." Ryan set the lamp on the bureau and read aloud, " 'Disregard the sheriff's warning of riot. His job is to keep order. Your job is to continue with the drawing as planned. Frank Blalock, President of the Cascade and Snake River Wagon Road Grant Company.' "

Ryan wadded up the telegram and threw it across the room. "Well, by God, what do you think of that?" He rubbed his face with both hands as if trying to make sure he was awake. "Yes sir, what do you know about that?"

It took a moment for Babs to understand the full significance of the wire, then she jumped up and ran to him. "We're back in the game," she said. "Old Mandell knew what he was talking about." She put her arms around Ryan's neck. "We're going to make the deal with Rand after all."

He picked her up and whirled her around, then put her down and she kissed him, a long, passionate kiss, the kind of kiss that she had not given him since they had come to Mallard City because it stirred them dangerously. Masquerading as father and daughter, they had kept a tight rein on their feelings.

They forgot the door was open, forgot that Mandell was not asleep in his room. Both were lost in the moment, and both were surprised when Mandell, standing in the doorway, said, "What is this? What's going on?"

Ryan dropped his arms and Babs whirled away from him, both red-faced and as embarrassed as two children caught in the pantry with the lid off the cooky jar. Mandell stood leaning against the door casing, his face flushed. He was drunk, but not so drunk that he could mistake their kiss for a father-daughter caress.

"We just had a telegram from the company . . ." Ryan began.

But Mandell was not to be side-tracked. "You're not his daughter." Mandell stared at Babs as if he had never really seen her before. "Why hell, you must be his wife. Maybe you're not even married. You're probably just some woman he picked up to come here with him. You've lied to both me and the company."

He stopped, his gaze whipping from Ryan to Babs and back to Ryan, and then, drunk enough to lose his usual caution, he shouted, "I won't stand for these shenanigans, being lied to and all, and with you two living this way right under my nose. You're fired, both of you. You be on the stage in the morning. I'll run the drawing myself."

For a moment Ryan stared at the old man, dumfounded, finding it hard to believe he had heard right. Then he roared in a great rage, "You pious old goat! You've tried every whore in camp and you've done your damnedest to drink it dry, but you've got the gall to come in here and fire us."

"It's different with me," Mandell said with drunken loftiness. "I'm the company. I'm the boss. You're a hired hand. I say you're fired. The stage leaves early, so you'd better start packing tonight. I'm going to bed now. You'd better be gone before I get up."

Ryan glanced at Babs. She nodded, understanding what had to be done. Without a word Ryan took three long steps and swung his fist, a powerful blow that caught Mandell on his chin. The blow sent him reeling back into the hall His knees gave and he crumpled to the floor, whimpering, "Don't hit me again. Please don't hit me."

Ryan picked him up and, carrying him to his room, dropped him on his bed. "I've some things to tell you," Ryan said, "and you'd better listen damn good, then sleep off your drunk. We're going ahead with the drawing. You are not firing us. We will handle everything just as planned. That's what our telegram said to do. You will stay right here in this room. Babs will bring your meals to you."

Mandell had no fight left in him. He rubbed his jaw, saying as plaintively as a child, "You hurt me. You shouldn't have hit me."

"If I catch you out of this room," Ryan said, "I won't stop at hurting you. I'll kill you. From now on until the drawing is finished and we get our money, I'm running this shebang. You understand? I'm the boss, not you."

He left the room and shut the door. Babs was waiting in the hall, her face mirroring her anxiety. She whispered, "There's hell to pay now, isn't there?"

Ryan nodded. "I didn't see any other way. I'm like Rand. We're too close to pulling this deal off to let it get away from us. If I have to kill the old bastard to keep the deal alive, I'll do it." He took Babs' hand and led her back to his room and sat down on the bed. He didn't say anything for a time, but stared thoughtfully at the wall across the room.

Babs stood looking down at him. Finally she said, "Well now, your majesty, just how do we play the last hand? If you kill Mandell, we're finished. The sheriff will have us in jail pronto. If you don't, and if Mandell gets to the telegraph office, he'll wire the company and maybe get the sheriff to come and arrest us." She shook her head. "I think we've got trouble."

"No," Ryan said. "I don't think so. At least, it's trouble we can handle. Mandell stood up to Plug Tully and the sheriff, but he won't stand up to me, not after I hit him. He's the kind who operates on bluff, using the idea that he represents the company. That won't work with me and he knows it. I think he'll stay in his room and let us go ahead. Be sure he gets his meals. If he does ask about me, tell him I'll eat him alive if he leaves his room."

"You think you can work that all week?"

"No," Ryan answered. "We can't keep the lid on that long."

"And what about Rand?" Babs asked. "He's too jumpy after what happened last night to wait more than a day or two."

"I'm thinking," Rand said. "If we quit our job tonight after the drawing, and if we ride out of the country, no one will guess we made a deal with Rand. We haven't committed a crime yet. By the time they figure out that we handed Rand the Cross Heart, we'll be gone. The point is Rand won't tell, so I think it's a fair bet they'll never know what happened. They'll think we ran out because we were scared of the mob. We'll leave a note saying that."

"So tonight's the night," she murmured.

"It's got to be," Ryan said. "Right after breakfast you go find Rand. I'd do it, but that mob of settlers would murder me. They won't bother you. Tell Rand I'll meet him back of the house tonight as soon as the drawing is finished. You have the horses saddled and ready to go. Tell Rand to have the money and I'll give him the papers to the Cross Heart as soon as he hands me the dinero. Then we'll be on our way. We'll ride all night. Tell Rand that if he cheats me in any way I'll kill him."

"I think he knows that." Babs hesitated, then she said, "We've been careful ever since we got here to give Mandell no reason to suspect us of not telling him the truth. Now that he knows, is there any reason I shouldn't finish the night sleeping with you? I need you. I've got along without you for a long time."

Ryan laughed softly. "No reason at all. Blow the lamp out."

CHAPTER XX

Johnny woke with the feeling that he had been asleep only a few minutes. The tent flap had been thrown back and daylight was streaming in. Somebody was standing there. When this finally got through to him, he grabbed his revolver from where he had laid it in the grass beside his head and sat up.

"Hold on," the man said. "Hold on. I'm Ed in case you're plumb blind."

"Sorry." Johnny rubbed his eyes. "I just knew someone was there and I figured it was Chauncey Ryan. For some reason I've had a crazy notion I was going to kill him or he would kill me before this was over."

"It may happen," Neal said angrily. "I've just had a wire from the company. They're going ahead with the drawing."

So that was what had got Neal out of bed so early, Johnny thought as he pulled on his boots and picked up his hat and gun. He clapped his hat on his head and shoved his .45 into the holster as he stepped out of the tent.

He had never seen Ed Neal violently angry, but now he sensed that Neal was seething in such a rage that it would take very little to tip him over the edge into doing some act of violence that he would regret later. He wondered what had brought this on. It must have been something more than the fact that the company was going ahead with the drawing.

Johnny had no intention of throwing any more fuel on the fire. He asked carefully, "Had breakfast?"

"No."

Johnny glanced briefly at Neal's stone-hard face, then said, "Let's go see if Ma's up."

"Read this first." Neal handed him a wadded-up telegram. "I couldn't sleep last night, so I went to the telegraph office as soon as it was daylight. That wire was waiting for me. I figured I'd get you up and we'd talk about it. I guess there ain't nothing we can do, though."

Johnny flattened out the telegram. As he read it, his anger soared, not from the actual message as much as the tone of the wire. Now he knew why Neal was so furious. "You attend to your business and we'll attend to ours. Yours is to keep order and protect our men. Ours is to continue with the drawing. We have wired Chauncey Ryan to that effect. Frank Blalock, President of the Cascade and Snake River Wagon Road Grant Company."

Johnny handed the telegram back to Neal. "The stinking know-it-all has done it now."

"It's just like a cheating company that wants a quick profit and don't give a damn about its responsibility," Neal said. "They'll spend a lot of money putting this scheme across and selling their lousy tickets to gullible idiots. They stand to make half a million dollars, but they can't wait to wind it up."

"Let's go see if we can get breakfast," Johnny said.

"Ma was starting a fire in her range when I came by her tent," Neal said. "Billy was cutting wood in the back. I don't know whether Ann Dillon's up or not."

They moved along the street toward Ma's Kitchen, Johnny glancing obliquely at Neal. Anger was still in the sheriff, the belly-deep anger that smolders in a man, but Johnny thought he had cooled off enough so there was little chance now that he would lose his self-control. Talking with Johnny had been a safety valve for him.

"It's like we were saying last night," Johnny said. "It would serve the company right if there is a riot. We've done all we can."

"It ain't that simple," Neal said grimly. "People in the county and even in the state won't know everything that's happened. Not that I figure on running for sheriff again, but I'd sure like to leave office with a good taste in my mouth, and with folks knowing I'd done the right thing. Now if Ryan and Mandell are murdered by a mob, I'll get blamed no matter what I've done to stop it."

Johnny nodded, knowing that Neal was right.

If the company had been willing to delay the drawing for a few days, or if Mandell was left in charge and Ryan fired, the settlers would have been mollified and probably would have drifted off and followed the same aimless pattern they had followed for years. Now Johnny hesitated to think about what they'd do when they heard that nothing was changed, that the drawing would go ahead exactly as planned.

Before they reached Ma's Kitchen, Neal said, "You know, I was sore when I got that wire in Piute asking me to come here. I didn't think the drawing amounted to much and I figured to go fishing with Chick Robbins. Our plans were all made.

"You see, my wife was out of town and it was a good chance for me to get away. Well, Mandell made a mistake sending for me, but I'm glad he done it. I didn't have any business sending you down here."

It was an apology of sorts. Johnny gave him a quick glance, thinking that Ed Neal was ashamed of his lack of responsibility, and he realized now that Johnny had been through a hell of worry before he had arrived. At least Johnny had not sent for the sheriff, and that was a source of pride to him.

"All I can say is that I'm glad you're here," Johnny said.

"Two heads are better than one," Neal said. "I

guess you can also say that two guns are better than one. What I aimed to say when I started was that I'm going to be glad to get out of office when my term's up. You're young, but you're the natural one to run. If you decide to tackle it and I can help you, all you've got to do is holler."

"Thanks," Johnny said as they turned into Ma's Kitchen. "I might try it at that."

Ma looked up from the range. "Well, if you ain't the early birds. Ann's still asleep, Johnny. I figured as tired as she was, I'd best let her sleep as long as I could."

"She could use the sleep all right," Johnny said. "You look all in yourself."

"I am." Ma swiped at a strand of gray hair that dangled against her forehead. "I figure this ain't gonna last forever. Maybe I'll make enough so I won't have to work so hard when I get back to Piute." She turned her gaze to Neal. "How about it, Ed? You hear from the company?"

Neal nodded. "We're going on with the drawing."

Ma sniffed. "Fools! Well, what will you boys have?"

"Flapjacks and bacon," Neal said. "Coffee right now if it's ready."

"It's ready," Ma said. "I put a pot on as soon as I started the fire."

They ate in silence, both men thinking of what lay ahead. Ann still had not come in when they finished eating. They paid for their meals and left the tent, Johnny carrying Dillon's breakfast. Neal strode beside Johnny, saying nothing until Johnny unlocked the jail door and opened it. Dillon stumbled out into the early morning sunshine, shivering.

He looked at Neal as he took his plate. "You the sheriff?"

"That's right," Neal said.

"When are you taking me to Piute?" Dillon demanded. "This here place sure ain't no jail."

"Won't be long." Neal shot a glance at Johnny. "Think he'll like the county hotel in Piute?"

Johnny shook his head. "Naw. He's the worst complainer I ever saw. Nothing suits him."

"I can tell him one thing," Neal said. "He's getting better grub down here from Ma than he'll ever get in Piute."

"That so?" Dillon seemed surprised. "Who cooks for the prisoners in Piute?"

"Ma does when she's there."

"And when she ain't there?"

"My wife."

Dillon sighed. "I guess you ought to know. I reckon you have to eat it all the time."

"That's right," Neal said.

Johnny hunkered down beside Dillon while he ate. Neal roamed around Johnny's tent and circled the jail twice, too nervous to sit still. As soon as Dillon finished eating, Neal said, "Lock him up again. We've got to go see Ryan and Mandell, I guess, though I ain't looking forward to it."

Johnny jerked a thumb toward the door. Dillon stood where he was, glancing up at the clear sky. Then he looked at Johnny and Neal. He said, "If you'll just let me sit here in the sunshine, I sure would . . ."

"Oh, no," Johnny said. When he had shut the door on Dillon and snapped the padlock, he said, "That bird has the damnedest ideas about what a prisoner's entitled to. Yesterday he wanted me to get him a horse and start him out for Piute. He'd go right to jail, he said."

Neal laughed shortly. "He's a real dreamer, ain't he?" Then as he turned toward the company office, he added, "I guess I ought to be ashamed of myself, but I keep thinking a bad thought. I wish Dillon had plugged Ryan when he shot at him."

"Yeah," Johnny agreed somberly. "It would have saved a lot of trouble."

They found Ryan eating breakfast by himself in the kitchen. He said jovially, "Come in, gentlemen. What can I do for you?"

Johnny, looking at the man, disliked and distrusted him more than ever. A cat that had just lunched on a canary could not have looked as smug as Chauncey Ryan did at that moment.

"Where's Mandell?" Neal asked.

"Sleeping it off."

"The woman?"

"The woman?" Ryan looked blank for a few seconds, then he said, "Oh, you mean Babs? She took a walk after she got my breakfast." Ryan leaned back in his chair, a taunting grin on his handsome face. "Well if you haven't heard from the company . . ."

"We've heard," Neal interrupted coldly. "That's why we're here. Go ahead with the drawing, but if anything looks out of line, or if you provoke the settlers . . ."

"Not me," Ryan broke in. "Babs, neither. We'll be very careful. Don't forget I was the one who got shot at. Tonight I expect protection."

Neal's pulse was pounding in his forehead. He glared at Ryan for a moment, then wheeled and stomped out of the house. Johnny followed him. When they were outside, Neal said, "That bastard is running a sandy of some kind. He's just too smart for his britches."

"Cute and careful," Johnny said. "If he'd do something we could arrest him for, I'd throw him in with Dillon."

"And slip Dillon's gun back to him." Neal shook his head. "He won't. Not until it's too late for us. By the time we figure out what's happened, he'll be a long ways down the road. You said Bradford didn't have any evidence to back up his claim about Ryan, but just on general principles, I'd guess he's right all the way."

"It's a good guess," Johnny agreed. "I'm going to see Bradford. Or O'Leary if I can't find Bradford. He ought to know what the company's answer is. Maybe he can calm the settlers down."

"Go ahead," Neal said. "I'm gonna try to get some sleep. I sure didn't get much last night. Just thinking about the company kept me awake. I guess I had a hunch all the time what the answer would be."

He turned away and strode along the street toward the tent hotels. Now that he was in Mallard City, the responsibility of enforcing the law was his. As he stared at the sheriff's back, Johnny wasn't certain that he ever wanted that responsibility. He had enough just being deputy.

CHAPTER XXI

Johnny was aware that the settlers were watching him as he threaded his way through the wagons, but he did not feel the pressure of their hatred as he had yesterday and the days before that. Today it seemed more a matter of waiting for something that had to happen, of neutrality, of indifference. These men would make up their minds about him and Ed Neal later. He grinned slightly as he thought about it. They were probably saying that the law just might be on their side.

O'Leary was not in sight around his wagon, so Johnny went on toward Bradford's. Then, glancing at Tebo Rand's wagon a moment later, he almost stopped in sheer surprise. Ryan's woman Babs was standing by a front wheel talking earnestly to Rand. Neither was noticing anything or anyone else.

Johnny thought he could have stopped flat-footed and stared at them and still they would not have known he was there. He slowed his pace, curious gaze on them. Babs was doing the talking, her mouth close to Rand's right ear. He was listening closely, nodding now and then as if he understood.

Johnny thought about them long after he had passed Rand's wagon. He didn't have the feeling that there was anything romantic between Rand and Babs. It was more as if she were telling him something of great importance that he had to do. Perhaps she had brought a message from Ryan.

This stirred another thought in his mind. If he had guessed right on that, then the next logical guess was about the message she had brought. It was understandable that Ryan had not come personally. Babs would not be harmed by the crowd, but Chauncey Ryan's appearance among the settlers might touch off the threatened riot.

Johnny was remembering what Norman Bradford had said. If Bradford's suspicions about Ryan were true, and if he had made a deal with one of the settlers for the Cross Heart, Tebo Rand might well be the man. Ryan, panicky because of Neal's efforts to have him fired, might have decided to deliver the Cross Heart tonight.

He was guessing. In fact, he was piling one guess on top of another, but Babs' presence here in the settlers camp did look peculiar. He walked on, knowing there was nothing he could do except to wait and see what happened tonight.

He realized suddenly he was lost in a maze of tents and wagons and horses. He had to ask twice before he found Bradford's camp. Again he had a strong feeling that the settlers were indifferent to him. He had made some headway, he thought grimly, if he had moved from a position of being hated to one of indifference.

Bradford was sitting on a camp stool, hunched over a chess board that he had placed on an upended box. He glanced up, recognized Johnny, and rose, extending his hand. "Good morning, Deputy," he said. "My wife and Delight are still in bed, so we haven't had breakfast. I'll start a fire and put on a pot of coffee if you'd like to have a cup."

"No, I just had breakfast." Johnny looked down at the chess men. He had seen a set once in Piute, but he did not know the game, and he was surprised to see Bradford playing it. "That's a queer game. You playing against yourself?"

"You might say that." Bradford laughed softly. "Sometimes I think we live a whole lifetime playing the greatest game of all against ourselves. Chess is a little different. There are some problems I like to work on and I don't know of anyone else in camp who plays. For instance, I'm trying to find out the least number of moves it would take to checkmate the king with two castles."

"Castles and kings." Johnny shook his head. "Don't sound much like our problem."

"Oh, but you're quite wrong, Deputy," Bradford said. "You see, we who are settlers are playing against the company, but we are short on power." He picked up a piece and held it in front of Johnny. "This is a castle, one of the more powerful men in the set. It's as if we had the castles taken from us when we started to play, but the company is playing with a full set." He made a savage gesture and his voice was suddenly angry. "We're handicapped. There's no justice about it, but that's the way it is."

"You're handicapped more than you know," Johnny said. "Ed Neal got the company's answer. They insulted Ed by telling him he'd better attend to his job of keeping order. They're going ahead with their job of continuing the drawing."

Bradford's face turned hard. "They're fools," he said. "Even with my help, I doubt very much that you and the sheriff can prevent a riot. It's been building too long."

"I thought I'd better tell you," Johnny said. "Maybe you can get the word out for the men to behave themselves."

"I'll try," Bradford said. "I promise nothing."

Johnny started to turn away, then swung back. "I saw something on my way here that I don't savvy. Babs was talking to Tebo Rand, real confidential like, and he was listening damned hard. It didn't look right to me. I wouldn't think she'd be here among the settlers."

Bradford swore softly. "It comes about as near to proving what we suspected as anything can. You see, we have had our suspicions of Rand for a long time. He is the only settler I've heard of who has counseled caution and has not believed that Ryan or the company or both were cheating us. He has said frankly that he believes Ryan and

Mandell are honest and we should go on that basis until we know different."

"I can't fault that attitude," Johnny said. "I wish you and your friends felt the same way. We wouldn't have any worries about a riot if you did."

"We don't aim to lie down and be rolled on," Bradford said sharply. "There's more to our suspicions. Rand has a good deal of money, and that sets him apart from the others."

"In the same way you're set apart," Johnny pointed out.

"That's true." Bradford gave Johnny a long, studying look. "That is, it's true I have more money than the average settler, but it does not set me apart in the way it does Rand."

Johnny shrugged. "Maybe not."

"I think you're trying to say something to me," Bradford said slowly, "and I don't think I like it. Or am I jumping at conclusions?"

"No, you're right and I don't think you will like it," Johnny said, "but I'm going to say it anyway. Ed Neal and me think you've got a little game of your own going, and that was the reason you started the story about Ryan being a crook."

"Now wait a minute," Bradford said. "You think I'm lying about him and Babs?"

"No, we don't think that," Johnny said, "but you could have kept your information to yourself, or come to me and Neal with it. Instead of that, you used your knowledge to get the settlers worked up. In other words, there would be no threat of a riot if you hadn't spread that story all over camp."

Bradford held his reply as he drew a pipe and a can of tobacco from his pocket and dribbled tobacco into the bowl. He tamped it down, his eyes narrowed, then he raised his head and looked directly at Johnny again.

"You're a pretty smart boy," he said. "Maybe a little too smart. Or are you quoting the sheriff?"

"I guess you'd say we got the same answer in our own way," Johnny said.

"Well then, since you're so damned smart," Bradford said softly, "would you tell me just what my little game is?"

"We suspicion that you want a delay so that most of the settlers, maybe all of them, will have to sell their tickets for what they can get, say ten cents on the dollar. You'll buy and they'll move on. You'll wind up with the whole shebang when the company finally gets around to finishing the drawing, so you'll get it at a bargain price."

Bradford's face, usually very genial, was sour. He asked harshly, "You see any crime in that?"

"No."

"All right then," Bradford said. "You have nothing against me. Just remember one thing. I'm the only man in camp the settlers look up to. I've got them right in the palm of my hand. In a matter of hours I can turn them into a howling, murdering mob that would go after you and the sheriff as fast as they would go after Chauncey Ryan."

"I don't think you'll do that," Johnny said. "You don't want any outside interference. If the riot was bad enough, the company could use its influence to have the governor send the militia in here. Maybe even close down the drawing."

"You're right," Bradford said. "I don't want any outside interference and I don't expect to work these people up into a murdering mob. I expect to help you and the sheriff keep order." He paused, then added slowly and deliberately, "I just wanted you and the sheriff to remember where you stood without me."

The threat was plain enough. Johnny said, "Now that we understand each other, is there anything else you have against Tebo Rand?"

"Why yes, we do," Bradford said, his tone friendly again. "We believe he bought only one ticket, so he must expect it to do great things for him. Since we started suspecting him of collusion, O'Leary has been watching him. Last night when the crowd broke up, Rand went to the company headquarters and talked to Ryan. O'Leary was outside, so he couldn't hear what was said, but on the face of it, we can only think the worst of him. Every other settler in camp considers Ryan an enemy and would never go to his office to see him."

"That's no doubt true," Johnny said, "but you have no real evidence."

"Remember this," Bradford said. "If Tebo Rand draws the Cross Heart tonight, you'd better look out. That's the lighted match which will set the explosion off."

"Then we will expect your help," Johnny said. "You be somewhere in the front of the crowd near the platform so they'll see you."

"Do we have a deal, Deputy?" Bradford asked. "You and me and the sheriff?"

"No deal," Johnny said. "For your own selfish interests as well as Ed Neal's and mine, we expect you to help us prevent a riot."

This time when Johnny turned, Bradford let him go. As he walked back to the road, the feeling of uneasiness that had been in him almost since he had first arrived in Mallard City became unbearable.

Late in the afternoon when Neal came into Ma's Kitchen for supper, Johnny told him about his conversation with Bradford. "I figured we guessed his game, all right. He didn't say so, but he looked as guilty as hell. I hope I did right telling him we were on to him."

"Just as well have all the cards on the table," Neal said. "We need him, that's sure." He shook his head. "So we wait. It won't be long now if my guess is right. You know, Johnny, I used to do a little mining when I was a young buck about your age. Sometimes we'd set a charge and fire it, but it wouldn't go off when it was supposed to. Then we didn't know what to do. That's about the way I feel right now."

"I feel the same way," Johnny said.

He felt something else, too. Norman Bradford might not be able to control the monster he had created, but he didn't mention his fear to Ed Neal. The sheriff had enough worries now.

CHAPTER XXII

The settlers began gathering in front of the platform before dark. Johnny, moving restlessly around the fringe of the crowd, had a strange sensation that time had stood still, that he was again seeing the events of forty-eight hours ago being played out before his eyes. Al Dillon would not be here, but in a crowd this size there would be a dozen men who could and would take his role.

The lighted torches on the platform threw the same weird, smoky light into the darkness; there were the same shifting shadows that made it difficult to identify a man at any distance. Plug Tully's men were lined up along the front of the platform, guns on their hips, eyes on the crowd.

Chauncey Ryan and Babs were on the platform with the wheel of fortune, the huge glass fish bowl, and the map of the Cascade and Snake River Wagon Road Grant. George Mandell was not in sight, but he had not been to any of the previous drawings, so that, too, was the same as it had been.

As the crowd grew and it was time to start the drawing, Johnny began to see and feel differences between tonight and forty-eight hours ago. There was a sense of finality about tonight that had not been here two days ago. This time there was the complete absence of women and children. Another difference was the presence of Ed Neal. Tonight Norman Bradford and Chuck O'Leary were in the front row of settlers. Johnny felt sure Bradford would help, but he expected nothing from O'Leary.

The crowd was strangely silent, an ominous sign that underlined the loss of the holiday spirit that had been present to some extent at the other drawings. It was as if everyone here was waiting for the inevitable disclosure of collusion that was certain to come, and then the crowd would roll forward like a massive juggernaut, destroying everything before it. Even with Neal here, and with help from Bradford, Johnny was doubtful that anything would stop the mob, once it began to move.

Ryan held up a hand and began to speak, apologizing for the failure to hold a drawing the night before. He explained that the sheriff had cancelled it without giving any reason or excuse so that it sounded as if it were an arbitrary and unreasonable act on Neal's part. Ryan added that there would be the usual ten names and numbers drawn tonight.

Johnny, standing halfway back on the east side of the crowd, suddenly felt another difference. Chauncey Ryan was not his usual jaunty self. The flamboyance which had marked his performance before was completely gone. He was tense, he used no more words than were necessary, and his arms, normally alive with motion, hung stiffly at his sides. He made no effort to sell more tickets; he even failed to announce that additional tickets were still available.

Ryan gave the wheel of fortune a spin. Babs drew a name from the fish bowl, then turned and handed the slip of paper to Ryan who glanced at it and called, “Chuck O’Leary.”

Ryan motioned to the girl. “Draw his number, Babs. Let’s see how lucky Mr. O’Leary is.”

Babs reached into the wheel of fortune and drew out a number. Ryan took it, shouted, “411” and turned to the map. “You have drawn twenty acres one-half mile east of the lake, Mr. O’Leary. Better luck with your next ticket.”

A noise like a great sigh rose from the crowd, the first sound Johnny had heard except for an occasional whisper. There was a nervous shuffling of feet, then a slight forward movement toward the platform.

So it went for nine drawings, no one getting any land of real value. Now, with only one name and number still to be drawn, Johnny felt tension grow until he wondered when it would snap. He was certain it would happen in a matter of seconds, or minutes at the most. He hurried toward the platform to stand beside Neal, the fingers of his right hand wrapped around the butt of his gun.

For some reason Ryan was moving very slowly, or at least it seemed so to Johnny. Ryan gave the wheel of fortune an extra spin, moistened his dry lips, and shouted, "All right, Babs. This will be the last drawing for tonight." She turned to the glass bowl, and Johnny had the impression that Babs, like Chauncey Ryan, was moving very slowly.

The girl slipped her hand into the bowl, drew out a name, and handed it to Ryan. He glanced at it, then called, "Tebo Rand."

Again the men shuffled their feet and edged toward the platform, and suddenly Johnny realized he had not seen Tebo Rand. He wondered if the man for reasons of his own was not here. There was no sigh from the crowd this time, not even a whispered comment of any kind.

This absolute silence from such a large crowd was the worst omen Johnny could imagine. The crowd reminded him of a great panther, ready to spring, muscles tense. He had no illusions about what was going to happen. If Rand drew the Cross Heart, all hell would break loose, and he was reasonably sure, after what Norman Bradford said about Rand, that it would happen.

Ryan said nothing and stood motionless as Babs made her selection of numbers from the wheel. She handed the paper to Ryan and began edging toward the rear of the platform. Ryan glanced at the number and called, "49." He turned to the map and added, "The Cross Heart, gentlemen."

Johnny and Neal pulled their guns as Bradford wheeled to face the crowd. He raised his hands and shouted, "Easy, boys. Easy." Neal had already given Tully and his men a nod. Their guns were in their hands before Ryan had called the number.

For a few seconds nothing happened. Johnny could see only a blur of faces in front of him. No one moved and it struck him that they were frozen. They had expected this to happen, and still they had hoped it wouldn't. Certainly every man here had expected to draw the Cross Heart. It was a strange silence that lasted only for an instant and yet seemed to go on and on, the haunting kind of silence that sometimes comes when a great storm has shaken the earth, and stops, and then breaks out in renewed violence after the moment of stillness.

The silence was broken by a tremendous roar that went up from the crowd. No words. Just the primitive sound of the wilderness, of hundreds of voices joining together in a cry of murderous hate and fury, then the crowd moved straight toward the platform like an avalanche. Johnny and Neal fired over the heads of the crowd, but even the thunder of guns was lost in the roar.

Tully and his men held their ground as long as

they could. They were firing into the settlers, not over their heads. Several men went down, but the pressure from the rear was so great that no one in front could possibly have held the crowd back. The men who had fallen were trampled underfoot, then Tully's men broke and ran, all of them clearing the corner of the platform except Tully.

Plug Tully didn't get away. He was one of the most hated men in camp because he had done his best to terrorize the settlers from the first. It may have been that the crowd was willing to let his men escape, but it wanted Tully's blood. Someone—neither Neal nor Johnny ever found out who the killer was—drove a knife into Tully's chest. Two of his men were beaten, but got away, and the other three were not caught. They were never seen around Mallard City again.

Johnny and Neal couldn't see what was going on and had no idea what had happened to Ryan and Babs. The crowd moved in so that Johnny and Neal were pinned against the platform. Bradford was on the platform, grabbing settlers as they leaped up beside him, talking to them, pleading with them to listen to reason.

The wheel of fortune was knocked over in the melee, and the glass bowl slipped from the man's hands and broke into a dozen pieces. Other men leaped at the map and cut it to ribbons with slashing knives. The settlers, normally quiet and law-abiding men, were crazy with hate and fury. Johnny, using his elbows and shoulders in his effort to break through the mass of humanity that surrounded the platform, thought that he had been right. Norman Bradford had created a monster he could not control.

The milling crowd on the ground gave way and Johnny broke through, Neal behind him, calling, "Look out for the men who were shot."

O'Leary, who had somehow been shoved to the far side of the platform, bellowed, "Tully's dead. He's been knifed."

Then, for some strange reason, the fury went out of the mob. Bradford, calling for restraint and common sense, was able to make himself heard above the hubbub. Someone else shouted, "Where did Ryan and the girl go?" Another man bawled, "They ain't nowhere around here." Then a third, "Fan out. We'll find 'em and we'll hang 'em good and high."

"No," Bradford shouted. "You've done too much now. When do you think this damage can be repaired enough to go on with the drawing? It's our loss, not the company's."

Someone shouted, "You ain't stopping us now, Bradford. We're gonna get 'em and hang 'em."

Johnny spotted the man standing a few feet from him. He struck the fellow across the head with his gun barrel, driving him to his knees. "Shut up," Johnny said. "You'd better listen to

Bradford before you get a rope on your neck."

"That's right," Neal said. "You hang Ryan and the girl and I'll arrest the bunch of you for murder."

Neal was on the platform beside Bradford, his gun in his hand. His hat had been knocked off, his hair disheveled, and his shirt torn, but now he stood apart from the crowd, his gun an effective argument. The racket died down, and Bradford urged, "Go on back to your camps. Rand will never get the Cross Heart. We'll get another whack at it."

"We'll find out if it was a crooked deal," Neal added. "It looks as if it was. I'll get hold of Mandell and make him call for an investigation. We'll get a fair deal for you, but you'll have to let the law do it."

Silence then, men's feet scraping around in the broken glass on the platform. Finally someone said, "We've been fools to bust everything up this way." And another man, "We'll be here till Christmas now."

Common sense began coming back to men who had been crazy only minutes before, and with it came regret and a sense of guilt, now that they realized they had hurt themselves more than anyone else except Plug Tully, who was beyond being hurt by anyone. The three men who had been shot by Tully's bunch and then trampled by the mob lay motionless where they had fallen.

Bradford said, "That's better. Let's have a look at our friends. If they're dead, it's your boots that did it as much as Tully's bullets."

The crowd fell back. Bradford and Neal knelt beside the injured men. Presently Bradford said, "They're hurt, but they're all alive. We'll carry them to their wagons. Their women can take care of them."

The crowd could be controlled now, so Neal wouldn't have any trouble handling the situation without Johnny. He reloaded his revolver, dropped it into his holster, and slipped away into the darkness, wondering if he had lingered too long.

Johnny did not believe for one minute that Rand had honestly drawn the Cross Heart. There undoubtedly was collusion, and if Rand got away now, there would be more trouble as soon as the settlers thought about it. Once Ryan was out of camp and Tebo Rand had the deed to the Cross Heart, neither Johnny nor Ed Neal could prove that Ryan and Rand had made a crooked deal.

CHAPTER XXIII

Johnny hoped to find Chauncey Ryan and Tebo Rand in or near the company office. If they weren't there he had no idea where to look for them. Neither man nor Babs would tarry in Mallard City any longer than necessary, so it was Johnny's guess they would meet at the old ranch house, exchange money for the deed to the Cross Heart, and be on their way.

Johnny realized there was a possibility that the exchange had already been made. If so, Rand likely was gone, and Ryan and Babs wouldn't stay here very long, perhaps only to change clothes and saddle horses.

The front room of the ranch was lighted. It was the room which served as an office, and as soon as Johnny saw the lighted windows, he breathed a sigh of relief. Apparently they were still there. He didn't run because the sound of pounding feet might alarm his quarry, but he moved as fast and silently as he could, drawing his gun as he approached the house.

He went through the front door and stopped, flat-footed. The room was empty. For a moment he stood motionless, disappointed. He had been so sure he would at least find Ryan here. He considered searching the house, but he heard no one. He had a hunch the house was as empty as this room. If Ryan and Babs were here, they would be making last-second preparations to leave, and he would hear them.

Johnny wheeled out of the house and into the darkness, rushing back from the fingers of light that fell through the open door and the windows. If Ryan and Babs had left Mallard City, the chance of finding them was close to zero because the surrounding country was big and empty. Tebo Rand would be out of the reach of the sheriff's office because he could show a deed to the property, and no one could prove he had not obeyed the letter of the law in obtaining it.

Johnny was halfway around the house when he caught the murmur of voices ahead of him. Both belonged to men. He was not too late after all. He moved on past the rear of the house as silently as he could so as not to alarm them. A moment later he was close enough to hear what they were saying, although it was too dark to make them out.

"I haven't got time to count the dinero," Ryan was saying, "but I will count it when we get a little ways from here. If there's a dollar missing, I'll hunt you up and kill you."

"You're a suspicious son of a bitch," Rand said angrily. "Give me the deed. I've got my wagon and team back here a piece. I've got to be moving. You were slow getting here, seemed to me."

"Here it is," Chauncey Ryan said.

A match flared and Johnny, quite close to them now, was surprised that Tebo Rand risked a light. The tiny flame showed him taking a quick look at the deed. Obviously neither man trusted the other. Johnny called, "Hook the moon, both of you. You're under arrest for conspiracy to commit fraud."

The match went out immediately. A gun roared, Ryan's gun, Johnny guessed, and he fired at once, hoping to get Rand who had hunkered down with the deed. Johnny jumped to one side as Ryan's gun sounded again, the stabbing finger of powder flame probing the darkness. He would be on the move, too, Johnny thought. Chauncey Ryan was certainly a veteran who had survived more than one gun battle.

Johnny went down flat on his face and emptied his revolver, firing low and spreading his shots so that if Ryan had moved to either side, he would have a chance of hitting him. He rolled over twice, then reloaded and remained motionless, eyes probing the darkness as he waited for some indication that one or both of the men were still alive.

He felt reasonably sure that he had nailed Rand with his first bullet because he had fired the second after the match flame had winked out; he had placed the man's big body in that brief moment when the match was still burning.

At this distance he could not have missed unless Rand had moved before Johnny fired, and he didn't think Rand could have done it. But he had no idea whether he had hit Ryan or not.

Johnny continued to wait, hardly breathing as he wondered if Chauncey Ryan was taking this opportunity to crawl away, or was waiting for some sound, some movement, that would give him a target. Johnny heard horses coming from one of the tent stables; men were running from the platform, one with a lantern that bobbed up and down in the darkness as he ran.

It was Chauncey Ryan who broke first, shouting, "Go back, Babs. Go back." He leaped up out of the sage brush a few feet in front of Johnny and started to run. Johnny, still on the ground, tipped up the barrel of his revolver and fired at the shadowy figure. He felt the buck of the Colt against his palm as powder flame slashed out from the muzzle of his gun, he heard Ryan scream in pain, and he knew that this time he had put the man down.

Johnny waited until the men came with the lantern, Ed Neal and Bradford and O'Leary and others, then he rose and walked slowly forward as Bradford caught up with him. In the murky lantern light he saw that Tebo Rand was dead with a bullet in his chest. Chauncey Ryan, lying thirty feet away, lay on his back in the sage brush. He had two slugs in his belly.

In the moment of life that was left for him, Ryan whispered, “Take care of Babs.” Then he was gone. The deed to the Cross Heart was still clutched in Rand’s right hand. An envelope stuffed with greenbacks was in one of Ryan’s coat pockets.

“I guess that’s proof of collusion,” Bradford said with satisfaction. “How about it, Sheriff?”

“It’s all we need,” Neal agreed. “You’ll get another chance to draw the Cross Heart.”

Johnny strode to where Babs sat her saddle, frozen by shock, the reins of a second horse in her hand. In a minute or so Ryan would have been on that horse and the two of them would have been gone, the darkness swallowing them.

Johnny holstered his gun and put his hands up to Babs. “Get down, Babs,” he said gently. “You’re not going anywhere tonight. Ryan is dead.”

She let him help her to the ground. Johnny said, “You men take care of these horses. Rand’s team and wagon are out here somewhere.” With an arm around Babs’ waist, he guided her through the darkness around the house and into the lighted front room. He eased her into a chair, asking. “Is there anything I can get you? I’ll start a fire and make coffee if you want it.”

“No, I don’t want anything,” she whispered. “I guess you know I’m not Chauncey’s daughter. What will I do, now that he’s dead?”

"I don't know," Johnny answered, "but looks like Ryan would have had something figured out for you. He must have known he was playing for big stakes, including his life."

"He knew," she said dully, "but he still didn't expect to die."

"A man like him never does," Johnny said.

Suddenly she broke down and began to cry. Johnny pulled up a chair and sat down beside her. He held her hand and patted her awkwardly on the shoulder, knowing there was nothing he or anyone else could do for her. Later, and it seemed a long time later to Johnny, she wiped her eyes and drew her hand away from his.

"I'm all right now," she said.

She was still wiping her eyes when Ed Neal came in. He drew up a chair and sat down in front of her. He asked, "Feel like telling us about it now?"

She nodded and wiped her eyes again. "There isn't much to tell that you don't know. I've been a thief and a crooked card player since I was a child. Chauncey was a con man and a crooked card player, too. Together we made a good team. I loved him and I did anything he wanted me to. We worked out this scheme with Tebo Rand, thinking that the $10,000 he was to give us would set us up in an honest business. Rand's name and Number 49 were never in the glass fish bowl or the wheel of fortune. I held them so it was easy to give them to Chauncey at the right time. I'm good enough with my hands so it wasn't hard to fool you and make you think I had drawn them."

She took a long breath that was close to a sob. "The only other thing is that Mandell is upstairs in his room. He's in bed. He caught us last night and Chauncey hit him and told him he'd kill him if he didn't stay in his room. This morning he tried to sneak out of his room to get to the telegraph office, or maybe go after you. Anyhow, Chauncey gave him a bad beating. He'll be in bed several days. I'll look after him. You don't need to worry about me hurting the old man."

"I'll go look at him in a minute," Neal said. "You stay here."

Neal jerked his head at Johnny and stepped outside. Johnny followed him. Neal said, "You done a damned good job tonight. I should have thought of what they'd do and realized that if they got away tonight, we'd have a hell of a time proving anything, but I couldn't think of anything except getting that mob cooled down. All I can say is that you're a good lawman."

"Thanks, Ed," Johnny said. "I'm glad it's over."

"It ain't entirely over," Neal said. "I've got to get back to Piute and I figure I'll go in the morning if Mandell ain't too bad off. I don't look for no more trouble. I'll take Dillon with me and we'll see how he likes a real jail. I'll send another wire to the company and this time they'll have to do something. I'll have Mandell send a wire confirming mine if he's able."

"Babs?"

Troubled, Neal said, "Hell, I don't know what to do with her. It don't look to me like we've got any case. It was Ryan's game, not hers. I'll let her stay here with Mandell. It'll be up to him if he wants to press charges, but the way he likes pretty girls and the way she can manipulate a man, she'll have him on her side in about three days."

Johnny nodded. "Or less."

"You go see Ma and Ann," Neal said. "Tell 'em what's happened because they'll be worried after hearing the shots. I'll leave you in Mallard City until you think you don't need to stay any longer. I figure Ma will be here as long as the crowd's here and that'll be a while. It'll take the company some time to unwind the mess that mob made tonight." Johnny started to turn away until Neal laid a hand on his shoulder. "That Ann now. You know, it strikes me she'd be an asset to Piute."

"She's one asset I aim to bring along," Johnny said.

"Good." Neal grinned. "I hope you do. Now get moving."

Johnny wheeled away and started to run toward Ma's Kitchen. He didn't have the slightest doubt what Ann would say.

Center Point Large Print
600 Brooks Road / PO Box 1
Thorndike, ME 04986-0001 USA

(207) 568-3717

US & Canada:
1 800 929-9108
www.centerpointlargeprint.com